F. TENNYSON JESSE

was born at Chislehurst, Kent, in 1888, on her father's side the great-niece of Alfred, Lord Tennyson; on her mother's side descended from Cornish seafarers, until her grandfather made a fortune in coal. After studying art at the Newlyn School of Stanhope and Elizabeth Forbes in Cornwall, in 1911 she began a career as a journalist, writing for *The Times* and the *Daily Mail*, and when war came she was one of the few women journalists to report from the Front.

In 1918 she married the playwright H. M. Harwood, and throughout their long married life they collaborated on several plays. All seven of her own plays were produced in the West End, the most famous of which were the wartime success *Billeted* (1917), and *The Pelican* (1924). Fryniwyd Tennyson Jesse published three collections of short stories and her very first, the famous tale *The Mask* (1912), has been translated and performed dramatically on stage, film and television. She also published poems, belles lettres and a notable history of Burma. She was a brilliant criminologist, editing six volumes of the Notable British Trials series, her *Murder and its Motives* being acclaimed by authorities in this field.

Of the nine novels she wrote, *A Pin to See the Peepshow* (1934) – televised by the BBC in 1972 – is perhaps the best known, whilst *The Lacquer Lady* (1929) is critically considered her greatest work of fiction. Both are published by Virago. F. Tennyson Jesse travelled widely and had dual homes in France and England. She died in London in 1958, leaving behind her a prodigious body of work, the breadth and versatility of which distinguish her as one of the most talented British writers of the inter-war years.

110654177

CAPTAIN
LOVEL

F.T.J.

MOONRAKER

BY

F. TENNYSON JESSE

WITH A NEW INTRODUCTION BY
BOB LEESON

Virago
London

*This book is dedicated to Captain I. Rice, Master
and the crew of the yacht 'Moby Dick' with the
friendship of the author and in memory of two
winters at sea with them.*

Published by VIRAGO PRESS Limited 1981
Ely House, 37 Dover Street,
London W1X 4HS
First published by William Heinemann 1927
Copyright © F. Tennyson Jesse 1927
This edition © The Public Trustees
The Harwood Will Trust, 1981
Introduction Copyright © Bob Leeson 1981
Printed in Hong Kong by Colorcraft Limited

This book is sold subject to the
condition that it shall not, by way of
trade or otherwise, be lent, re-sold,
hired out or otherwise circulated
without the publisher's prior consent,
in any form of binding or cover other
than that in which it is published and
without a similar condition including
this condition being imposed on the
subsequent purchaser. This book is
supplied subject to the Publishers
Associated Standard Conditions of
Sale registered under the Restrictive
Trades Practices Act, 1956

British Library Cataloguing in Publication Data

Jesse, Fryniwyd Tennyson
Moonraker. – (Virago modern classic).
I. Title
823'.912[F]   PR6019.E57
ISBN 0-86068-186-6

INTRODUCTION

In 1912, the English Review published a short story by an unknown writer, F. Tennyson Jesse. A powerful piece, it caught the eye of an established dramatist, H. M. Harwood, who saw its possibilities as a play. He wrote asking permission to dramatise the story and addressed the letter, without a second thought, to Mr. Jesse.

This kind of assumption must have figured often in the life of Fryniwyd Tennyson Jesse, as it does to this day in the lives of professional women who do not think it necessary to signal their sex like a red flag in front of an early model car. Indeed Fryniwyd perhaps thought that by signing herself neutrally F. Tennyson Jesse, she might, as a professional, avoid special consideration or rather condescension.

She became a successful writer. Not a best seller, but anyone first published in 1912 who is writing TV plays in 1958, with scores of works in between may safely be called a success. Anyone who worked as a war writer in two world wars, 1914-18 and 1939-45 may claim to be unique. Her story of San Demetrio, the torpedoed tanker whose crew re-boarded and sailed the ship home was a World War Two classic. She accomplished, in fact, more than most writers, but she could not be free of such remarks as that of the critic A. C. Ward: 'Her books are more intensely alive than those of any women now writing in England.'

'Compliments' of this kind, like being called Mr. Jesse, were no doubt part of her life. No doubt in the life of work she was to share with that same H. M. Harwood, she learned to take them with a laugh. Her writing shows from time to time a sardonic sense of humour. But what these things represented: that a woman cannot be 'herself', or rather can only secure acceptance in the world of work and creativity by denying part of herself, must have meant a great deal to her. Joanna Colenbrander, who worked closely with Tennyson Jesse for much of her writing life, says of her: 'She was a skilful, amusing, clandestine sort of feminist, never tired of getting in an adroit plea for the dignity and independence of womankind. This would come out innocently but devastatingly in her books, letters and conversations, though she never joined any movement for this or any other cause. She was always a loner.'

One of her best known works, *A Pin to See the Peepshow* expresses the outrageous demand of a woman to live as she chooses. But, when it comes to spelling out the ambiguities and ambivalences in the life of a woman who seeks to be everything she feels she can be, not just those things society will accept, then F. Tennyson Jesse makes her clearest statement, not in a novel, not in a play and not in an essay. She makes it in *Moonraker*, which at first sight is a typical 1920s romantic adventure. It was published in 1927 when you could get away with writing such stories for adults and children at the same time and illustrate it with your own line drawings of ships and pirates.

She was a much better sailor than her clear model for much of the writing in the book – Robert Louis Stevenson. She knew a great deal about boats and seafarers and packed almost too much of it into the 160 pages of this tale. But into this seemingly unlikely context – the year 1800, Napoleonic wars, pirate ships, wrecks, French 'mounseers', Barbara Cartland ladies in Empire style, saying 'La, sir,' the reader finds a debate about what society does to women: 'You know, I feel sure as well as any of your sex, what is admirable in a woman. Gentleness, fragility, meekness. Even, if I may so express myself, a pleasing feebleness . . .' Or: '. . . . Health, strength and courage, are these of no avail, except in a man? Must a woman have a waist distorted out of all semblance to nature, have a timorous disposition, a squeamish sensibility?'

The reader finds more than this. Specifically within the four powerful chapters which form the denouement of this little book, there is an *embodiment* of woman's rebellion, which is unforgettable.

But *Moonraker* has yet another dimension to add to this message of liberation. Along with, and specifically linked to its feminism, is a cry for freedom for black people. Never before, and rarely since – until the most recent period – have these two freedom fights been so specifically and dramatically joined. That they should be blended in the work of an English upper-middle-class woman, descendant of sea captains, coal merchants and – yes – the ancient Poet Laureate Tennyson himself, is a remarkable thing. That they should be blended in a 1927 adventure about a sailor boy hero (shades of Marryat, Stevenson and Herbert Strang) is even more remarkable.

By the 1920s, the adventure story with a historical background, the product of decades of Victorian writing, was almost at its last gasp. Writers like Naomi Mitchison and Geoffrey Trease, who were to bring fresh life to the genre, both in spirit and writing skills, were not yet making their impact. As Geoffrey Trease was to write some years later in his essay in *The Thorny Paradise* edited by Edward Blishen (Kestrel, 1957):

'A new story in 1920 or 1930 tended to be a fossil in which one could trace the essential characteristics of one written in 1880 or 1890. The British must always win. One Englishman equals two Frenchmen, equals four Germans, equals any number of non-Europeans . . . the common people subdivide into simple peasants, faithful retainers and howling mobs. The Cavaliers were a good thing. So were the French aristocrats except for their unfortunate handicap in not being English.'

And, one might add, women were firmly kept in their place – a place which Naomi Mitchison was specifically to challenge in her novels of the Ancient World.

Moonraker, in 1927, was, to borrow an appropriate nautical metaphor, a shot across the bows of the old adventure story. It is a great pity that F. Tennyson Jesse has not previously been given credit for her single, but powerful contribution to change in this genre of story. For alas, to continue the metaphor, although this little story was published in the USA and Sweden, it then sank without trace. My own reading life, which began in the 1930s and encompassed almost every adventure story I could find, the good the bad and the ugly, never included *Moonraker*. So I can thank Virago for that.

Moonraker bites off more than it can chew, as a good many stories which challenge the status quo tend to do. And regrettably the author, steeped as she was in Cornish folklore, chose to write the opening chapters of the book as if they came from the mouth of a West country sea dog – and a very stagey old sea dog, too.

But once she settles down to her real purpose, she goes back to writing as F. Tennyson Jesse. From there on, the style is closer to the mark and when we reach the four chapter climax, it is memorable, both for the physical action and for the way in which the argument about men, women and human liberty is given full blooded, painful and exhilarating life.

Jacky, the sailor boy hero, with face and curls like a girl is given a future vision by a witch. He sees two faces, one sad, noble, black, the other handsome, sunburnt white – at first sight a man, but. then, perhaps a woman.

Captured by Captain Lovel, a real devil, the last of the pirates, Jacky begins to find his stereotyped loyalties are shaken – pirates are human. But more is to come. After further adventures he joins Toussaint L'Ouverture, liberator of Haiti in guerrilla warfare against the forces of Napoleon, and meets the grim black generals Christophe and Dessalines.

He fears them but adores Toussaint. The author goes no further than an acceptance of those black freedom fighters who seem most like the best whites. Her description of a Voodoo ceremony, comparing it unfavourably with the carnage aboard a pirate ship, marks the outer limits of her attitude, as does her picturing of Christophe and Dessalines as 'savage'. I make these points, of course, with considerable respect for the author and underlining how many light years she was in advance of the conventional literary attitudes of her day. In the 'sea-dog' passages she uses the word 'nigger', but where the author's own voice comes through it is always 'black' or 'negro'.

Certainly a writer who could put into Toussaint's mouth the following words, knew a thing or two. The black leader is referring to Raoul, liberal French nobleman, and smiles sadly: 'It is true he loves liberty, she is a goddess he admires. But we are not fighting for an ideal, Jacky: we are fighting for the actual liberty of our bodies, that they shall not be ill-used.'

But more is to come. Failing to rescue Toussaint, Raoul persuades Captain Lovel to take on board Laura, his sweetheart and another white woman, to the disgust of the pirate crew. As the ship sails away, the scene is set for the grand finale – a dramatic set piece in which the author shows all her playwright's skill. In these final chapters the ambiguities and ambivalences of the plot already aroused in the mind of the reader come out into the open. The tremendous climax to the book has been seen simply as a larger-than-life 'woman scorned' melodrama. But the trail laid throughout the book, as well as the explicit linking of denied female humanity with the slaves' revolt make the final statement quite unambiguous.

Jacky goes home, marries, settles down. But those two faces seen in the witch's vision, are always in his mind: '. . . a black face and a white one that was sun-reddened, and they were the faces of the two most real people he had ever known.'

Bob Leeson, London, 1980

CONTENTS

CHAPTER I

IN WHICH JOHN JACKA'S JACKY RUNS AWAY
TO SEA

NOW this is the yarn as Jacky Jacka, Big John Jacka's son, used to tell to Johnnie Jacka, his son. Jacky was a young lad when it all happened in the years of our Lord, eighteen hundred and one and eighteen hundred and two.

Young Jacky ran away to sea as his father, Big John, had done before him, for it was better to ship before the mast in a merchantman of your own free will, than to be pressed, as every likely-looking man might be pressed, into the King's service. All the Jackas were born sailormen ; every hair of ropeyarn, every drop of blood of Stockholm tar, and every finger a marline-spike ; and both Jacky Jacka and his son climbed through the hawsepipe to the weather-side of their own quarter-deck, where they ended in broadcloth frock-coats and top-hats that you could have seen your face in. The old man, Big John Jacka, had served in the

A

ships of the Honourable John Company, and
fought against the French and the Dons and the
Hollanders and the Portuguese, and Dyak pirates.
He started as an ordinary seaman and became a
chief gunner before he married a Bristol girl and
settled down with her, in a house with a window
each side of the front door, in Saltash, on the
Tamar. He knew Garden Reach and the Pagoda
Anchorage and the Hongs of old Canton, where
the flower boats with their silken curtains, and the
scarlet tea-junks with their towering poops, and
the hundreds of little sampans, and the bazaar
boats crowded with merchants, were all anchored
beneath the terraced go-downs in front of the
Forbidden City of Rams, and made in themselves
a whole city of colours and perfumes and a strange
wicked sort of music, enough to bewilder a poor
sailorman. But the yarn of young Jacky is stranger
than anything his father, Big John, had to tell,
even with the rum well in him. And Jacky's son
Johnnie raced in the China opium clippers, and
fought the yellow pirates in their junks with painted
eyes. He conned his vessel time and again through
the Sunda Straits ; he weathered typhoons and
defeated the wiles of the mandarins who didn't wish
their people to take opium, but he never met anything as strange as young Jacky Jacka met when he
was round about the dark island of the Caribbean.

Come to that, a strange thing happened to Jacky
before ever he left the West country. There was

an old woman called Tamsin True, who lived on the moor, and she was a witch. Jacky was a favourite of hers, for he had more than once driven off other boys when they were throwing stones at her. Jacky always had to do a deal of fighting on his own account, for the boys laughed at him because he was as pretty as a girl, with golden locks crisp as the shavings that curled up before the boat-builder's plane. His skin was rosy and his eyes of the greenish-blue of the deep water near the rocks. It was lucky for him that he was a fine upstanding little fellow, or he would have had the life teased out of him.

Well, one November, a pale fine misty day it was, Jacky got into a brawl at the grammar school, and the master told him he was sick of his ways and that he could leave for good, and Jacky threw the inkpot at the master and walked out and went up over the moorland road to cool down a bit. And he would have passed by the way to Tamsin's cottage if it hadn't been that there was a crowd of people before it, all of them calling out and shaking their fists and making a fine boutigo. They looked black as a cluster of flies against the white cottage.

Jacky struck across the bit of moorland and came up to the crowd, and saw it was made up of the people from the mining village near by. There was old Tamsin, behind her window, very pale, with her face looking as though it were drowning behind the thick greenish glass. Her mouth was mumbling and moving, but no one could hear her, for the thickness of the panes and the murmuring of the crowd.

A young woman with long black hair and wild eyes was holding up her baby in her arms, holding it up and out, and she was calling in a dreadful voice, over and over again, these awesome words : " *Mother, call your flock home ! Mother, call your flock home !* " Then all the crowd would echo her and shout : " *Mother, call your flock home ! Mother, call your flock home !* " This was a strange thing to Jacky, and he stepped over and took a look at the child, and he felt his flesh creeping on him. For that babe was covered from head to foot with crawling maggots that moved ceaselessly like water.

Jacky asked the meaning of this thing, and the father told him that Tamsin had a grudge against him, and that she had taken a fistful of churchyard earth and blown it over the babe, and that it had come out all over with the crawling things of the dead ; and that was why they were all shouting : " *Mother, call your flock home !* "

Jacky slipped round to the back of the cottage and got in that way, and said to old Tamsin : " You 've got to cure that babe, Tamsin, or they 'll knock seven bells out of you, that 's as certain as Christmas." And he opened the window and called out to the folk, who were getting ready to throw stones, and he said that Tamsin would lift the curse off the babe if none of them touched her. So they ceased their threatening, and Tamsin came out in the pale sunlight, and she looked like one dead herself, and every one but the young mother drew back from her. Tamsin muttered a spell over the babe, and lo ! it was all clean and white as a lily once more. Tamsin had called her flock home, though no one could say how she had done it. There were many witches in the West country in those days.

The crowd went home rejoicing, and Tamsin was rare and grateful to Jacky, for she had been in a powerful fright of stoning ; and she took hold of Jacky's chin and turned his face up and looked long into his eyes, till Jacky felt all wisht-like. " What do you see, Tamsin ? " asked Jacky.

" Oh ! " answered Tamsin, " *I see tall ships drowning in the green of thy eye, and dark deeds done in the black of it.*"

And she would tell him no more, but she made him stare into a bowl of water that she set in front of him ; and Jacky stared till the water seemed to go cloudy, as though some one had poured milk into it ; and then, in the middle of the cloudiness, he saw a face.

It was a long, lean, brown face, with a high nose and bright blue eyes, and brown hair that was brushed back, and at first he thought he looked at a man ; and then the clouds cleared away a little more, and he saw the neck and shoulders, and he saw that it was a woman, with lace and satin drawn over the breast, and the throat was red with the sun, but the shoulders were white. Then the

water in the bowl began to get all agitated and
heaved up in little waves like a sea, and Jacky only
got glimpses of pictures that formed and broke in
the breaking of the waves. He saw a cloud of
bright canvas and the spars of a vessel ; he saw
black smoke rolling from the mouths of cannon ;
he saw tattered strips of bright flags ; he saw high
green mountains with streams of clear water falling
athwart them ; and last, he saw a strange black face,
and the eyes were so sad that he shut his own
because of the pain they gave to his heart. When
he opened his eyes again the water in the bowl lay
clear and untroubled, and he rubbed his lids and
looked from it to Tamsin.

She asked him what he had seen and he tried to
tell her, but it was all confused in his mind as it
had been in the bowl of water. " Thou art going
on a voyage, cheild vean," she told him, " and
thou art going now," and more she wouldn't say.
Jacky thought of the schoolmaster and of the bottle
of ink, and thought of his father waiting at home,
with a look like thunder and a rope's end like
lightning, and he decided that Tamsin was right.
He climbed in at his bedroom window, did some
clothes up in a bundle, rowed himself across the
Tamar, and walked to Plymouth Hoe, where he
stood and looked down at the shipping in the bay.
By evening he had signed on in the brig *Piskie*
that was sailing next day for the West Indies and
the Spanish Main.

CHAPTER II

THE *Piskie* was a likely-looking brig, all white, with a sheer that made her look like a paring of the young moon when she lay riding to her anchor. Her skipper was her sole owner and a bachelor as well, and what he made he spent on her as though she were his sweetheart. Her decks were holystoned till they were as white as milk. Her brasswork fair dazzled your eyes, and she had suits of sails in her locker like gowns in a pretty woman's wardrobe. Her figurehead was of pure white, and a comely virgin she was, there is no denying. Folks said that at night, when he thought no one was watching him, Captain Billy Constant used to swing himself out over the knight-heads and down on to the bowsprit foot-ropes, where he was able to reach up and kiss her on the mouth. Jacky never caught him at it, so couldn't vouch for the truth of this.

She sailed from Plymouth in the misty November dawn, and Jacky saw the Hoe fall away and fade astern, and the green slopes of Mount Edgcumbe on the starboard quarter, and then they stood out to sea, and by evening the Lizard was astern, and the *Piskie* was lying over nicely, with a white bone in her white teeth and a singing through all her rigging that made the heart glad. Young Jacky

7

was happy as a lord, and the only thing he felt
sore about was that the days of the pirates were
over ; for though there were plenty of French
privateers dodging about the Caribbean, and a
few pirates as well, they were poor things to a boy's
fancy compared with Captain Kidd and Morgan
and Blackbeard and the rest of them.

The *Piskie* kept sailing, never starting a ropeyarn, and taking a gale in her stride like the beauty
she was ; she made her southing quickly, and when
she was out of the westerlies she picked up the
N.E. trade, and then was sailing free on a south-
westerly course, as happy as a queen. She headed
for the Mona Passage, for she was bound for
Montego Bay with a general cargo. Billy Constant
smacked her taffrail after a habit he had, and told
her she should have a new coat of paint and fresh
gilding on her gingerbread work, for beating her
own best passage.

And then, one brassy noonday, when she was
in 26 N., 65.20 W., the mast-head look-out reported
a sail on the starboard bow. They were getting
into waters where they might expect to meet a
French privateer, and Billy Constant scanned the
stranger closely through his glass when she showed
up over the rim of the world. She was a tall
rakish-looking craft, close-hauled on the port-tack ;
through his glass he could see the bone in her teeth ;
she was coming along in fine style. Like the *Piskie*,
she was a brig, but higher sparred, and, so Billy

Constant made out as she drew nearer, far more heavily armed. He called his mate, Mr. Nankivell, and consulted with him, pacing up and down the poop. The stranger drew nearer, but still steering an easterly course, which would take him well astern of the *Piskie*; but while Billy Constant and his mate watched, they saw the stranger alter course. He bore away and steered S.E., and Billy Constant and Mr. Nankivell turned and looked at each other. " By gum! he 's after us ! " said Billy Constant.

" He is that," said Mr. Nankivell.

" We 'll have to run for it," said Billy Constant. So he up-helm and hung out every rag the *Piskie* possessed and steered S.S.E.

For three hours the *Piskie* fled and the stranger pursued, overhauling her steadily, for he had some three knots speed of her. The day was full of a blowing brightness like the soul of a youth, the vessels passed from sunlight into the cloud shadows that dappled the face of the waters. Once a squall came up, and a driving mist, and the *Piskie* hoped she might slip away and be lost, but when the weather cleared, there was the tall stranger lying over in the smother, her leaping forefoot shining in the sun, and her copper sheathing a-dazzle, like a streak of flame. Soon she was within firing distance, and she sent a cannon ball into the *Piskie's* main-mast, carrying away the yard and the port rigging, so that the whole raffle was banging about against the gaff of the spanker.

Billy Constant sung out for a couple of men to go up and cut everything away, and then he hit her on her taffrail, and told her for the Lord's sake, and his sake, and her own sake, to show what she was made of. And she was made of the sweetest oak, with a copper bottom as clean as a hound's tooth, but that didn't save her when a cannon ball blew a hole in her that you could have sailed her own longboat clean through. The next ball got her in her powder magazine, and she blew up astern and Captain Billy Constant with her, and a good thing too, for the heart would have been broken in his breast if he had lived to see her go down. The pirates boarded her forrard and looted all they could get ; the few men that were left they took prisoners, and among them the lad Jacky.

Jacky was taken along to the cabin of the pirate captain, and a fine cabin it was, taking up the whole of the stern, with square windows and rich panelling of polished wood. It was the hour of sunset, and the light lay on the water, turning it red, and the reflection of it struck like flame on the ceiling and filled the cabin with a ruddy glow.

The Captain was a handsome young man, with a long lean brown face and a high nose, and deep wrinkles around his eyes, which were bright blue and innocent as a babe's. He looked as little like

a bloody murderer as any one you could think of.
And the queer thing was, that Jacky had a feeling
that he had seen this face before, but he couldn't
remember where, and the more he puzzled over it
the less he could catch his memory, which was
beating round in the back of his mind like a moth
in a lantern. The pirate wore great gold ear-rings,
and his name was Captain Lovel, which is a West
country name, and his mouth speech sounded
homely to Jacky. He told Jacky he was to be his
cabin boy, and that he would be treated well as
long as he behaved himself, and that he would get
a rope's ending if he didn't, just the same as in
any decent vessel afloat.

The brig was christened the *Moonraker*, and
Captain Lovel had taken her from the Yanks after
a great fight, when she had been on her way back
from the River Plate with specie and hides. She
had been built at Salem for the north-west fur
trade, and so she was heavily armed in case of
Indian attacks, and made a fit craft for a pirate.
She was copper-bottomed, and she carried single
topsails, t'gallant-sails, and royals, and set stunsails
on both masts. She also set every kind of Johnnie
Green that she could crowd on ; she looked a real
lady when she was all dressed up in her best, clad
in snowy muslin from head to heel. Her bowsprit,
with the jibboom and flying-jibboom, was the hell
of a length, and it was steeved right up so that the
tip of the flying-jibboom looked to be above her

foreyard. She was painted black, with a white band and square black gunports, and she flew the Jolly Roger from her spanker-gaff when in action, just like the pirates in the story-books. Her lines were as sweet and her heart as sound as any vessel's afloat. Poor Billy Constant couldn't have loved the *Piskie* better than Captain Lovel loved his ill-gotten *Moonraker*. You might have thought it would have made him understand another man's love of his ship, and be sorry for what he had done, but that was not Lovel's way. He saw well to her armaments, and kept her fit to commit her murders. She carried swivel guns on her bulwarks, and twenty-four cannon kept well shotted with grape or canister or langrage. Her quarter-decks were loopholed for musket fire, and pistols, muskets, boarding-pikes, and boarding-nettings were always ready to hand.

She was a sweet ship to steer, and Jacky, who had been born with his hands on the spokes of a wheel, could not but love her when the Captain tried him, to see whether he could stand his trick, which Jacky could, as well as an older man. He did not want to forget the *Piskie* and poor Billy Constant, and he grieved for them both. He felt he would never forgive Lovel for that killing, and the sight of the *Piskie's* sails, lying flat over on the water, darkening as the swell took them more and more, like the wings of a wounded gull, stayed in his mind. Piracy was all very well to read of, and

pirates were doubtless very good fun to fight when
you beat them, but he had never imagined them win-
ning. It made it all ugly and cruel instead of a great
adventure. And now he was in a pirate vessel
he might be forced to take part in these evil doings,
and if they won, he would have to see honest sailormen killed and taken prisoner, and if they lost, he
would be taken prisoner himself, and then perhaps
he might be hanged from a yardarm as a pirate.
It was all strange and confusing, and he tried to
hate Captain Lovel ; he knew he couldn't hate the
Moonraker.

But it wasn't so easy to hate even the Captain.
He was short and sharp, as was only natural in a
skipper to a cabin boy, and there was something
frightening about him apart from that ; yet you
couldn't hate him. He kept even his mates at a
distance, instead of being free and easy and jolly,
as you would have expected in a pirate ship. The
only man he ever spoke with alone in a friendly
way was old Red Lear, the bo'sun, a great hairy
man, who had known the Captain ever since he
was a nipper, so the other men said. They 'd been
picked up all over the Atlantic, some by shanghai-
ing, some by capture, and some because they were
natural born robbers and murderers, and had
wanted to ship in just such a vessel.

Lovel kept his word, and treated Jacky no worse
than he said, and even a trifle better ; for once,
when the mate was going to flog Jacky for spilling

the molasses all over him when he was waiting at the cabin table in half a gale, the Captain took the yoke-rope from him and flogged Jacky himself, and it must have been to let him off lighter, for the blows hardly stung him, though the Captain had been known to half take a man's back off. The discipline on that craft was sterner than on any law-abiding merchantman. You might have been in a ship of the line or an East Indiaman.

The *Moonraker* dodged about those waters for a while after sinking the *Piskie*, trying to waylay one of the many American ships that were trading constantly back and forth, bringing rich cargoes of nankeens and pepper, coffee and wine and tobacco, and taking iron and hemp and sailcloth and flax, all good things for another ship to get hold of by fair means or foul. She gave chase to one for a day, but the other vessel showed her a clean pair of heels, piling on her shining towers of cotton canvas. There was no going near Captain Lovel after that. He hated being out-sailed.

Jacky could understand that. He was praying with all his heart that the other craft would get away safe, and yet he hated not catching her. Besides, she was a Yank, and the *Moonraker* was British-owned now, even if by a pirate, so of course she ought to have won.

CHAPTER III

CAPTAIN LOVEL told his plans to no one, but after this he put the *Moonraker* about, and they headed on a sou'-sou'-westerly course, and the men said that he was now off on the plan that had been in his head all along, which, said they, was going after the buried treasure of Captain Kidd on the island of Tortuga. Treasure was a good word in Jacky's ears, especially as no one need be murdered to gain it, for all the blood spilt over the gold of Captain Kidd was dried long since. The *Moonraker* lay over to the breath of the Trade, and Jacky was happy as the blue water fled by.

The Captain was leaning over the lee-rail one evening, when Jacky brought him up his shot of rum, and after he had drained it he pulled Jacky beside him and pointed to the white foam that slipped and turned away from the vessel's way. It was a great patch of foam, like a spread of curdling cream, and the sun, which was setting in a blaze, as though the heavens were a-fire, threw the shadow of ship and rigging right over it like a net ; and this shadow shortened and lengthened with each plunge the vessel gave.

" That 's the soul-ship," says the Captain gruffly.

B

Jacky looked in amaze, but the Captain went on speaking, more as if to himself than to Jacky.

" Every ship carries her soul-ship alongside, I reckon, and when she dies that dies too, and often it goes to sleep before, when there 's no sunlight or moonshine, or when there 's not enough way to make the foam bed for the shadow ship to lie on. But she 's only asleep, waiting to jump out. I wonder sometimes if I lose my ship whether I lose the soul of her too."

Jacky didn't know what to say to this, so he said nothing, only took the empty rum glass from the Captain's hand, for it seemed as though he might drop it. The Captain sort of came-to with a start, and gave Jacky a great clap on the back and told him to be off, and Jacky went, but he could tell the Captain wasn't angry, for he was smiling, not the way he smiled when he frightened you, but simple and merry, as it might have been any one. And after that Jacky always felt the Captain was a bit different from what he 'd thought, and was beginning to forget the cold rages he 'd seen him in, and the things he 'd done, when it all began over again.

The *Moonraker* was steering W.S.W., bound for the Turk's Island Passage, when she sighted a French merchantman on her starboard beam, sailing merrily along with the wind on his port-quarter, and Captain Lovel began to pace his poop with quickening steps. He fired a warning shot and ran up his flag, and all through the ship there was excitement.

The Frenchman plainly intended to fight, for instead of running away, he held on. Jacky clutched the rail and stared with all his eyes, his heart beating like a bird in his breast. The enemy was a Frenchman, and he had always been told to fight the French, but, on the other hand, his own vessel was but a pirate, and every manjack on board of her liable to be hanged if he were caught by a decent sailorman of any nation, including his own ; and he thought for a miserable moment of Billy Constant and the lovely *Piskie*, and he realised that though this was a Frenchman, with doubtless a Froggie in command, yet she was a beautiful ship and her commander must love her. He wished with all his heart that he were on a British man-of-war and could fight the stranger with a clear mind. Out of the corner of his eye he saw Captain Lovel standing abaft the wheel, and he saw that the Captain was tense as a swung catapult, his chin up and his eyes blazing and his fists clenched, and a bright colour on his high, lean cheek-bones. Jacky's heart went out to him ; he was a scoundrel and a murderer, but there was something wonderful about him, something alive and splendid.

There was, by now, no doubt that the Frenchman had decided to fight, and both vessels began to manœuvre to get the advantage of being to windward. For a couple of hours they dodged about, their copper sheathing leaping above the green water, their sails now bright in the sun, now cavernous with shadow. The *Moonraker* bouted ship, and came up to the wind close-hauled on the starboard-tack, for the Frenchman was coming up close-hauled on the port-tack, edging his nose to the east, while the *Moonraker* was trying to outwit him by swinging up northward. Then the Frenchman went about when the *Moonraker* was to leeward and astern of him, and so both were steering due north, and the *Moonraker*, having the speed of the Frenchman, began to draw ahead, edging up and up, so that if the two vessels held on long enough she was bound to get the wind-ward position.

By now Jacky was holding on to the rail with both hands, and he had forgotten everything in the excitement of the manœuvres ; he beat the rail as though he had been Billy Constant, to try and flog the *Moonraker* along faster. Every stitch of her cloths drawing to their bolt-ropes, and the lines of her beautiful clean hull helping her, she drew ahead, till at last she went about on to the port-tack with a crashing of her boom and a rattling of her gear, and a thudding of men's feet on her decks as they raced to the braces. Jacky's throat was dry and his eyes starting out of his head ; now they would cross the Frenchman's bows and get to windward. A crashing of guns already shook the whole framework of the *Moonraker* and the sea was thrashed into a fountain of foam, but only one ball hit the Frenchman, slicing off a few feet from his bulwarks. The rolling clouds of smoke floated away, yellowish black against the brightness of the day, and the Frenchman answered the *Moonraker*, not only with bursts from his guns, but also by the same manœuvre of going about on to the port-tack. But the *Moonraker* was standing nearer the wind and she was faster than the Frenchman. She drew up well to windward of him and closed with him. Not all of the Frenchman's cunning seamanship had availed him against the *Moonraker's* greater turn of speed.

With a grinding and a crashing the vessels locked, amid great bursts of flame that flared oddly red and sullen against the clear heavens. The smoke rolled thick and suffocating. The *Moonraker* was, of course, always in battle trim ; her decks were cleared and sanded as soon as a sail was sighted ; every man knew his station and was ready, either with boarding-nets and pikes or with ramrods and powder, long before the moment of engagement was upon them. The *Moonraker* clung on to the bigger merchantman like a terrier on to a bull. The Frenchmen fought like demons, though their vessel was not near as heavily armed as the *Moonraker*, but once the grappling-irons were out the fighting was hand to hand, and nothing better could any man have wished to see. It was Jacky's first taste of a good fight, and he could not but

enjoy it, a thing not to be wondered at. He felt
a bit sick at his stomach when he looked at the mess
afterwards, but after all that could not be helped.
The sinking of the *Piskie* had been a dreadful
business, but this was a Frenchman, though
only a peaceful trader, and we were at war with
Boney. And what a fight he had put up ! All
the Frenchies fought well, but the one that stood
out most was a young man, not in the dress of a
sailor, who fired his pistols till he had no bullets
left, and then whirled a sword round his head like
a flail. Jacky was always catching sight of him
through the changing clouds of smoke.

After the French captain was killed, and the
ship down by the head and settling fast, and every
one thought the fight was over, this young man
seemed to go mad with rage, and came charging
down the slope of the deck, straight for Red Lear,
who dodged him, and whirled a belaying-pin with
such good aim that the blade of the young man's
sword snapped off close by the hilt. Red Lear
went in to finish him then, for the Frenchman made
to go on fighting with the stump. In another
moment Red Lear's belaying-pin would have
crushed Frenchy's skull for good, but Captain
Lovel all of a sudden seized hold of Red Lear
from behind and threw him on the deck. The
young man went staggering on, blinded with the
blood from a scalp wound that was pouring over
his face, and the Captain jumped after him and

seized him, and spoke him fair, and the young man seemed to crumple up suddenly in his arms.

Red Lear came up in a towering passion, for though an old man he was bloodthirsty, but Captain Lovel ordered him to bring water and bandages, and when Frenchy's head was tied up he was carried on board the *Moonraker*. Two of the wounded jumped into the sea sooner than let the pirates come near them, three more agreed to sign on with Captain Lovel, and the rest were dead or dying. The ship had a cargo of Lyons silks and velvets, of claret and eau-de-vie, and some pipes of port. Captain Lovel only let his men broach a couple of casks of the claret. After all the loot had been taken, the last of the pirate's crew left the Frenchman, and none too soon, for a few minutes after she gave a last shudder, and sticking her nose down, while all her loose gear roared and rattled through her from stern to stem, she dived under the stained and littered water and was gone. That was a sight Jacky never grew used to, seeing a proud vessel founder, no matter what enemy of England had sailed her.

The *Moonraker* lay hove-to for the night, and kept anchor-watch ; the crew slept like the men they had sent to the sea's bottom. Next day she resumed her W.S.W. course, but with shortened sail. Even pirates, Jacky found, needed to rest sometimes, and the *Moonraker* had been in two engagements in the span of half a score of days.

She sailed along quietly, making good what damage
she could while under way, always keeping her
nose set for the Turk's Island Passage, some
hundred and fifty miles away. That would take
her, with her reduced sail, forty-eight hours or more,
and forty-eight hours is two whole days.

A night's rest had restored the young Frenchman to himself. He had been the only passenger
on board the merchantman, and he had been
bound for the island of San Domingo. He
seemed in a great taking and distress of mind.
He was the handsomest young man you ever clapt
eyes on, with black hair and a pale face, and great
dark eyes like the eyes of a man that sees visions.
With his head neatly bandaged next day, and his
dress all put to rights, he seemed a goodly youth,
though Red Lear growled at him. Red Lear
never rightly got over the feeling that he 'd been
done out of killing him. Soon Red Lear hated
him more than ever, for it was plain that the Captain
had taken a great fancy to him, such a fancy as he
had never been known to take to any human being
before. Red Lear had a natural distrust of anything soft, and besides, he was always powerfully
jealous of the Captain ; it was a joke amongst the
rest of the crew. Jacky found the young man was
called Mounseer Raoul de Kérangal, and he was to
mess with the Captain in the after cabin. They
had a long talk there, for the young Mounseer
spoke English very well, but Jacky only caught

snatches as he went in and out, and couldn't quite
tell what it was all about. Raoul talked very
eagerly, and seemed to be urging something, and
the Captain listened without saying much, his chin
on his hand, looking at the young man thoughtful-
like out of his blue eyes.

CHAPTER IV

IN WHICH JACKY AND THE CAPTAIN BOTH
LISTEN TO THE MOUNSEER

IT was a strange day indeed, that one that followed the fight. There was a feeling of something new abroad, and no man could say what it was. Red Lear might mutter to himself, but none could catch what he said. Captain Lovel looked different ; somehow he seemed very quiet and yet more alive. He was strange, and so was everything aboard the *Moonraker*. For one thing, it was the first time since Jacky had known her that she lolloped along as though she were lazy, instead of stretching herself like a greyhound. There was quiet in her rigging instead of the perpetual thrumming as of a giant harp to which she was wont to sing her way across the seas. Only the creaking of the yards and the slow swish of the water slapping her sides broke the leisure of the day : men lay and nursed their wounds, or slept off their violence, and in the cabin, alive with the flickering crescents reflected from the waves, the Captain and the young Mounseer sat and talked. Jacky waited on them ; took broth to the Frenchy, who lay very pale but animated in the bed-place, his head wrapped in linen and his eyes flashing beneath the white folds. You might have thought he would have been tired, what with the cut on his head, and

24

now with so much talking and imploring, but nothing seemed to tire that young man ; his tongue hung on an oiled hinge, and the oil was so fine and sweet that not only the Captain, but Jacky, as he came in and out with dishes and flagons, felt entranced by it. It seemed that this young Mounseer was a disciple of somebody called Roussoo, who believed in the equality of man, the same that the Frenchies had been in such a mess about several years past. And there was some one on the island of San Domingo, one of the French blacks, that Moun- seer Raoul admired even more than he admired Roussoo, who was dead anyway.

The young Mounseer belonged to a society called " Les Amis des Noirs," which Jacky found out meant " The Friends of the Blacks," and he hated Boney almost as much as an Englishman did, be- cause he said that Boney was double-crossing this black man. Mounseer Toussaint l'Ouverture, the black man was called, and he was the Governor- General of San Domingo, and young Raoul thought no end of him, that was clear as daybreak.

" Why, sir," says the young Mounseer to the Captain, " I swear to you that Toussaint l'Ouver- ture is the blacks' saviour. And that the blacks want saving, what man of heart can deny ? I was a boy staying on my uncle's plantation when the revolution of '91 broke out. Toussaint was a slave there ; he got me away, and my uncle's steward and his wife and family, hid us in the woods and provided food for us, and at last got us away in a boat to North America. Then he joined the blacks and became their leader ; he put a new spirit into them—his own. And after that, the cause of human liberty in San Domingo went ever onwards and upwards."

" Human liberty ! " says the Captain, " human liberty ! No man alive has liberty. Liberty, equality, and fraternity, that 's how the jargon goes, ain't it ? "

" That is the ideal of the human race," replies the young Mounseer, sort of stiff.

" Not aboard a vessel, leastways not in any craft of mine."

The young Mounseer seemed very upset by this, and began to talk harder than ever, but Jacky had no excuse for staying any longer in the cabin, so he didn't hear what it was all about. When he came in again, the Frenchy seemed to be pleading for something, and the Captain was walking up and down the cabin, with his chin sunk on his breast.

" If I do what you want," said the Captain, just as Jacky came in, and the young Frenchy had sunk back exhausted on his pillow, " you must give me your parole to come back with me. Suppose we try and rescue this black friend of yours and we fail, you 've got to come back aboard the *Moonraker*. Is that agreed ? "

" Why should you try and keep me ? " cried

Mounseer Raoul. " I shall never turn pirate, and I will pay you a ransom to let me go."

" Those are my terms," said the Captain, very short and sharp ; " you can take them or leave them."

" I have no choice," answered the other ; " I have to take them if I am to be in time to warn my friend. I give you my word to return on board with you."

The young man seemed suddenly to be tired out ; he closed his eyes and turned whiter than ever, and the Captain shouted to Jacky to bring a shot of cognac along, but when Jacky brought it he gave it to Frenchy himself, holding up his head with one hand and tipping the liquor down his throat with the other, as clever as a woman might have done. Then he shouted for two of the men to come and carry the young man up on deck ; pillows were arranged for him on the poop, and he lay there in the shadow cast by the spanker. Then the Captain changed course, and instead of holding on for Tortuga, steered S. by E. The men began to wonder and grumble, but none except Red Lear dared say a word to the Captain. Red Lear muttered something, but the Captain sent him for'ard with a flea in his ear.

By dusk word had flown from mouth to mouth that the *Moonraker* was heading for the Mona Passage, at the eastern end of San Domingo, between that island and the island of Puerto Rico.

This was an odd happening, and there was much talk and grumbling in the fo'c'sle of the *Moonraker*. There was no more talk of treasure or of Tortuga ; but instead the Captain watched and listened to the young Frenchman, walked the poop beside his couch, or sat and pored over charts in the chart-house.

The westerly set of the current helped the *Moonraker* well through the Mona Passage, but light and variable winds setting off and on the shore at different hours of the day and night made her take over three days to Cayes Jacmel. All the time they were sailing past a strange and terrifying coast, hung with beauty and richness, indeed, but so lofty, so uninhabited, save occasionally for a thin blue wisp of smoke, that it pressed upon the heart like doom. Here and there, along the margin of the surf, stood a row of grotesque tree trunks the height of a man, capped by swollen boles that looked like a series of heads set upon stakes. Jacky saw it with the odd feeling that he 'd seen it somewhere before, which he knew he couldn't have. High green mountains, with glittering streams falling athwart them.

CHAPTER V

NOW Cayes Jacmel affords but little shelter, and only coasting schooners call there, and that was just why Captain Lovel dropped his pick in those waters, for it was unlikely he would meet any vessel to cause him disquiet. He ran the *Moonraker* in past the reefs and sandbanks, through the southerly entrance, steered her westward, and brought up east of the village where the reefs gave her some shelter from the heavy set of the sea. There the *Moonraker* lay and licked her wounds, and while she was being put to rights the Captain and young Raoul sailed westerly in the longboat to the town of Jacmel, taking young Jacky with them. There was a watering-place on the western side of the bay, between two white cliffs, and all the water-barrels were filled anew, and the men stripped on the sandy beach and bathed in the surf ; it was all like a picnic, and very pretty and nice.

Jacky had three happy days, for he was allowed much shore liberty by the Captain. The high white walls round the gardens were covered with bright purple and scarlet creepers. In the green forests that stretched up the mountains behind the town, hundreds of parrots flew about like streaks of green fire. In the streams laughing washerwomen stood slapping the clothes against the boulders ; so black and shining their legs looked, like dark pillars in the bright waters. It seemed a lovely island, and yet it still frightened Jacky in an odd sort of way. There were strange orange puff-balls that grew under the trees, unlike the fairy rings on the moors at home ; somehow these seemed more like demon rings, if you can imagine such a thing. Great fleshy-leaved prickly plants, that the Captain said were called cactuses, grew everywhere, looking as though they had been dreamed in somebody's nightmare, and once Jacky saw a bright green snake slipping through the undergrowth ; he gave a shout and ran to kill it with a stick, but some negroes working near caught hold of him with cries of horror, and afterwards they went down on their knees and bowed their heads on the ground and called out words that Jacky didn't understand, but that sounded as though they were praying to the snake hidden in the bushes. This was odd, for it seemed that the people of this island weren't heathen, only Papists.

A great Calvary, as Mounseer Raoul called it, stood up out of the town. Jacky was afraid of it ; it looked so mournful, and yet it was friendly too, for he knew that though it wasn't right to worship idols, yet this was an image of the Saviour. It was a strange country, but the people were friendly and polite, and gave Jacky fruit, and smiled at him.

Young Mounseer Raoul rode off on a mysterious

mission, and the two days and two nights that he was away, Captain Lovel was as fidgety as a woman. He came back all right, but very tired, and it seemed he had ridden for seventy miles to Port-au-Prince and back for news of his black man. Whatever the news was, it made them shake their sails out and up-anchor, and the *Moonraker* sailed due west to Cape Tiburon, twelve hours' sailing. Then she made a northerly course up past Cape Dame Marie, and kept on till she was well in the Gonaives Channel, where she hove-to.

Now Captain Lovel had no intention of going into the harbour of Port-au-Prince, wherein he might have met warships of many nationalities, so he hove-to until afternoon, when the westerly wind blows, and he ran before it till he was under the lee of the island of Gonave, where in a sheltered cove he brought up.

There was something queer about the whole business, thought Jacky ; this was a strange-looking island, and its people were strange, and as he lay in his hammock that night in the lee of Gonave Island, there travelled to him across the water a throbbing noise that frightened him, he couldn't tell why ; somewhere in the dark forests great drums were being beaten.

C

CHAPTER VI

THE next day, when the westerly breeze had
set in at noon, Captain Lovel told Jacky he
was to accompany him and Mounseer Raoul on a
shore expedition. You may be sure Jacky was
pleased, and that he put on a clean shirt and his
best blue neckerchief, and gave his shoes a polish.
They might be gone several days, said the Captain,
so he and the Frenchy took little valises, and Jacky
took a clean shirt done up in a handkerchief. A
very fine figure Captain Lovel made when he came
on deck. There was nothing of the pirate about
him now ; the big gold rings were gone from his
ears ; he wore white breeches and white silk stock-
ings and buckle-shoes and a dark blue broadcloth
coat with silver buttons. They all got into the
longboat, and she ran before the westerly breeze
into the harbour of Port-au-Prince, right into the
small basin of the inner harbour. Jacky was as
happy as a king. Lying in a great curve, the green
mountains were dappled with purple cloud-
shadows, like those that pass all day over the moor-
lands at home, and Port-au-Prince was a fine white
city, a little dirty perhaps, but what does a little
dirt more or less matter ?

Everywhere the royal palms stood in rows, like

32

pale grey pillars with green feathery tops. There were black boys along the quays selling bright-eyed monkeys and emerald parrots and piled-up fruits like all the wealth of the East. There were black women, with scarlet and orange turbans, and calico gowns cut out of rainbows; they smiled at Jacky, and rolled their white eyeballs at him from behind their stalls covered with wooden platters and granite-ware—jugs and basins and cups of rose and purple, green and blue. There were great piles of glossy green coffee-beans and pinky-grey cocoa-beans, where the little negroes sat and played, and wriggled their black fingers and toes in and out of the sliding heaps. Behind the market stood the cathedral; black women kept passing in and out. " Let us go in and see it," said Raoul, and the Captain broke into a laugh. " I thought you didn't believe in religion, all you new-fangled people." " We have discarded the old super-stitions," answered Raoul with dignity, " but it is very well permitted to retire a moment into a quiet place and commune with the great Spirit of the Universe." Then he burst out laughing, and stood looking all sort of shy and much less alarming than he had done just before. " Now I am talking like a book again, just as you told me I did, my friend; after all, why should I be ashamed of being human ? In Brittany, my mother worships in an old-fashioned church like this. Perhaps I wanted to think like she does just for one moment."

They all three marched up the high white steps
and entered the church, which was very dark and
quiet after the noise and clatter of the market-
place. It had wooden columns painted blue like
a strange moonlit forest of shady trees, and a blue
ceiling covered with gilt stars. Raoul knelt down
on the brick floor, and then a very strange thing
happened. Jacky was standing first on one foot
and then on the other, with his cap in his hand,
wondering whether a good Protestant would kneel
in a Papist church or not, for there was something
about this sweet spicy smell and the dimness and
the kneeling figures here and there which made
him want to, and yet he didn't wish to do anything
unbecoming an Englishman, when he heard a
clatter beside him, and there was the Captain down
on his knees, his sword sticking out behind the
soles of his upturned shoes, and his brown head
bent, apparently saying a prayer ; his face was very
red, and his lips moved a little without making any
noise. That was a queer thing, thought Jacky,
to see a man of blood thinking it did any good to
pray, but he went down on his knees himself and
thought for a moment or two about the grey Tamar
and the wind-flaws that travelled across it, and
the little white house amid the fuchsia bushes,
where an old man might be staring through his
telescope to catch sight of the sail that might be
bringing his son home. They soon all got to their
feet, looking rather silly, and Raoul remarked on

the superstition of a couple of negresses who were knocking their heads on the brick floor in front of a statue of the Virgin.

They went out again into the bright sunlight, and Raoul took them all to an inn which Jacky found was called a caffy, and there they all had little glasses of brown rum. Then the Captain said to Jacky: " Now, boy, you listen to me. Mounseer Raoul and I have come here to try and help this General Toussaint. He is the skipper of this island, and a damned good one too, it seems, and Boney is sending out the hell of a lot of ships and soldiers to lay him by the heels. We 've come here to try and save him and get him away in time. That 's all you need know. Do what you 're told, and do it damn quick, and leave the rest to me." Jacky pulled his foremost yellow curl and said : " Yes, sir." But Mounseer Raoul seemed to think there was a lot more to be said, and he told Jacky all of it, and Jacky listened, with the rum tingling down to his toes, and thought how fine it all was.

It appeared old Toussaint had taken the name of l'Ouverture, which means a doorway of opening, because he considered he had opened the way to liberty for his people. And so he had, said Raoul, not only for his people, but for the whole of mankind. For, said Raoul, liberty was the birthright of the human race, and Toussaint l'Ouverture was helping all men by helping the blacks in this island. Since he had become Governor-General, there had been no more revolutions or massacres, and before that, the whites had massacred the blacks and the blacks the whites, each in their turn. Toussaint was loyal to France, said Raoul ; he had driven out the English and the Spanish, and had helped the French General Laveaux, who thought no end of him, and had made him Commander-in-Chief. Wasn't this a great thing, asked Raoul, that a man could have been fifty years a slave and brought freedom and peace and prosperity to a people, and made himself a ruler ? And Jacky said, yes, it was, and why didn't Boney let Toussaint alone ?

"Ah, my little Jacky," answered Raoul, "but you see, the white planters and owners who live in Paris have got frightened ; they think the blacks are getting too much. And the First Consul is angry because he heard how Toussaint said : 'I am the Bonaparte of San Domingo.' So he ordered a great expedition to set sail from France against the island, and directly I heard of it, I shipped aboard the French merchantman which Captain Lovel sunk. I wished to get to San Domingo in time to warn Toussaint and take him away."

"But won't he want to fight ? " asked Jacky, and Raoul shook his head sorrowfully and answered : "I tell you the might of France is going against this little island. The veterans of the Alps, of Italy, of the Rhine, of the Nile, have been gathered together, under the First Consul's own brother-in-law, General Leclerc. What can Toussaint do against such an expedition as this ? I admire and love Toussaint, little Jacky, and still more the cause of freedom and humanity, but I would have you know that a French army can't be vanquished."

Jacky heard Captain Lovel give a little snort, so he didn't like to say anything for fear of disagreeing with the one or the other, so he pulled his curl again, and they all got on to three fine horses which were waiting for them outside the caffy. There was a black man in a shabby uniform holding the horses, and he whispered something to Raoul, who nodded, and then they all mounted and rode away ; the Captain and Frenchy together, and Jacky behind them.

Now they all three rode to a place called Ennery, above the Bay of Gonaives, where General Toussaint l'Ouverture had his country house, and they rode through jungle where strange flowers bloomed, all among quaint ferns and huge silk-cotton trees with roots where you could have built a hut between the silver arches ; and the air was full of a green light, and the little humming-birds hung at the lip of a blossom, their wings whirring so fast you could see nothing but a blur. The wild pigs broke through the undergrowth, pot-bellied spiders hung on the trailing creepers ; the green darkness seemed alive with things that listened and things that looked. It was very hot, and the sweat ran off Jacky and tickled him like the creeping of flies. Every now and then they came on a clearing where charcoal-burners were at work, and every now and then they passed through a tiny village of palm-leaf huts, where rice and canes grew, and the pot-bellied little piccaninnies played in the dust. They slept that night in a little village up in the mountains, and the fireflies danced like all the little stars of heaven come alive. That night again Jacky heard the drums, and he lay awake and listened to the strange sounds that rose and fell, swelled and died away, so that you couldn't tell at what point of the compass the drums were being beaten. Raoul turned over and said in a low voice to the Captain : " The blacks have heard there 's trouble coming. They 're gathering to the Voo-doo priests. Toussaint will be sad at that." Jacky wondered what the Voo-doo priests were, and suddenly fell asleep.

Next day, in the clear cool dawn, they rode down into Ennery. There, beside the river, was a long white house, with pillars all along the verandah ; it was set high above the white beaches that stretched in the distance down to the sea. They dismounted, and were given baths and changed their raiment, and presently they were told that His Excellency would see them. They were taken by a tall buck nigger, covered with gold lace, to a big room with a lot of little gold chairs. The light in this room came through the slats of the green shutters, and it was like the depths of the sea.

CHAPTER VII

IN WHICH JACKY MEETS TOUSSAINT L'OUVERTURE
AND RAOUL DE KÉRANGAL MEETS LAURA

A LITTLE black man, hardly more than five feet high, but gorgeously dressed, was waiting in this room.

Now, for the third time, the odd thing happened to Jacky, that thing which had happened when he first saw Captain Lovel, and again when he saw the green mountains and their glittering streams. He looked into the dark eyes of the black man who was standing there awaiting them, and he knew that somewhere he had seen those eyes before, and that they had been so sad that he had had to turn his own away.

They were not sad now, they were bright like enamel, but Jacky knew all right that these were the eyes that would be too sad to be borne ; it was as though a hand had stretched out and closed about his heart.

Toussaint l'Ouverture took off his plumed hat with great courtesy and bowed low, then he ran forward a step and seized both Raoul's hands and broke out into quick expressions of affection and pleasure, and Raoul seemed very happy and excited too. Jacky saw that this Governor-General had several front teeth missing ; he was ugly and sad-looking, like a sick monkey, and yet you felt he was a

great man, though he was as black as the Earl of
Hell's riding-boots. He wore a blue coat and a
scarlet cape that fell down behind from head to
heels ; he had great gold epaulettes and a scarlet
waistcoat and pantaloons, and red leather half-boots,
and a hat with a French national cockade and three
feathers, red, white, and blue, standing up out of
it like a palm-tree.

Raoul introduced the Captain, and the Governor-
General was very affable ; his manners were indeed
elegant, thought Jacky.   Then he and young
Raoul began to talk together very fast in French,
which Captain Lovel understood well, but of which
Jacky could only get a few words here and there,
but the upshot of it all was that the black General
found it difficult to believe what Raoul was telling
him. Toussaint said that the great French nation
was the friend of Liberty, and that his brother,
the First Consul, by which he meant Boney, was
the friend of Liberty too, and that neither could
ever break their word, and he trusted in them
implicitly. Raoul half-laughed and half-cried and
went on talking. " It is no good," Raoul said at
last in English to Captain Lovel, " he won't come
with us."   And Toussaint understood him and
laughed too, and his smile was so sweet that Jacky
forgot all about his being black. " I shall be ver'
well, my friends," said the General, in a funny
sort of English. " My people they will stand by
me, but there will not be war, no ; there is peace

now in my island." Then Raoul began again and urged him a lot more, but the General drew himself up, and he slapped his chest and he seemed to swell, and he thrust his right hand inside his fine coat just like the pictures of Boney, and he said : " No, no, I can't run away in your sheep ; there is no sheep built that is big enough for a man like me ! "

Then Raoul shrugged his shoulders and seemed to give up, and when Toussaint said : " Now, let us all go and have breakfast together, my friends," he just bowed. The great doors were thrown open, and they saw the dining-room, with a long table covered with glass and glittering plate, and a little crowd of gaily dressed people standing by the window.

" Here is a friend of yours," said Toussaint, and he smiled in a way that made you forget how ugly he was, and waved his hand towards a young lady in a peach-coloured dress of silk. Raoul stared for a moment as though he couldn't believe his eyes, and then he said : " Laura ! "

The young lady swept him a curtsey, and though her cheeks were blushing, her voice was as prim as a schoolmarm's as she said : " Your servant, sir." She was as pretty a piece of pink and white as a man long at sea could dream of : her eyes were grey and her yellow head lifted like a bird's on her little neck.

There was much talking and explaining and laughing. Madame Toussaint, a nice old black lady, in a gown of rich silk, but a manner as simple as you please, had to embrace Raoul, whom she had not seen since she made up his food for him when he escaped, and then she had to exclaim on how he had grown and how handsome he was, and to ask him if Mamzelle Laura hadn't grown a lot too. Every one was polite and nice to the Captain, but of course no one knew him as the Toussaints and Miss Laura knew Raoul. They all sat down to table, and the Captain drank a lot but ate little, and his eyes burned like blue flames in his red face. Jacky sat at a side-table with the Toussaint children, and they all laughed and chattered and enjoyed themselves very much. It was a slap-up meal, though General Toussaint only ate a little fruit and drank water, but there were rich wines and rare dishes for every one else.

Jacky soon found out that Miss Laura, who came of a noble French family, had been a little girl in the house in America where young Raoul had been taken when he escaped from the massacre eleven years earlier. Jacky thought she was the most beautiful young lady he'd ever set eyes on, and Raoul seemed to think so too ; they talked and laughed a lot together. There was an elderly lady in grey silk, a Mrs. Pounsell, with her, and it seemed they had both come to stay with the Toussaints to show them the way ladies and gentlemen behaved in Philadelphia.

After the meal Jacky and the children went out

and rode races along the meadows. Much later, young Raoul came out of the house and called to Captain Lovel to bathe in the river with him, but the Captain came out on to the verandah and shook his head and refused very short and sharp, and Raoul shrugged his shoulders and came down to the river alone. He called to Jacky to join him, and they bathed together in the clear water where the great lilies held up their cups to catch the sunlight. Jacky had a sudden feeling that this was the best day of his life, which he often felt had been full of trouble, as it is only natural to feel at fifteen. He forgot all about pirate ships, and about Boney, and thought that this was what life was like, with a cool river and green shade and a sky and sea clear as crystal, and parrots that flew past, and lizards that shone like jewels and sat puffing out golden bubbles beneath their chins. But that evening, as every one was collecting in the great room with the gilded chairs before going into dinner, a black man arrived, galloping, at the verandah, and he and his horse were both streaming with sweat. He brought news that a great fleet had been sighted approaching the Bay of Samana ; over sixty sail of war-vessels. Toussaint stood for a moment like an image in black stone when he heard the news, then he shouted out in a great voice, and ordered horses to be brought round. He came up to Raoul, and pressed both his hands, and then he took Captain Lovel's hands and pressed them as

well. " Ah ! my friends," he said. " We can't
fight against so many ; we must make peace. I
will ride to the Bay of Samana at once, and see if
I cannot persuade the French general that we do
not mean war. My poor people, I cannot see them
plunged in bloodshed once again."

Toussaint l'Ouverture, at the head of his bodyguard, his two trumpeters behind him, started off on
the long ride across the mountains to the Bay of
Samana in the east, and Captain Lovel and young
Raoul and Jacky Jacka rode in his train. And all
night long the beating of the native drums sounded
through the blackness of the forests.

CHAPTER VIII

IN WHICH JACKY MEETS CHRISTOPHE AND
TOUSSAINT MEETS ISAAC AND PLACIDE

THE days blew past Jacky like spindrift, for everything was new and strange, and he could understand but little of it. After several days and nights when, so it seemed to Jacky, they hardly ever rested, they arrived at the headland above the Bay of Samana. There, on the shining floor of water, lay the mighty French fleet. Great first-raters, of three decks and over a hundred guns, frigates like greyhounds, corvettes that rested lightly as gulls on the water. All the pomp of France in their gilded ports and carven sterns, there they lay, the black mouths of their guns silent but threatening. Their decks were crowded by men in blue and men in scarlet, their boats, with oars that flashed back and forth in the sunlight, were busy between their high black sides and the shore.

Toussaint stood gazing on this scene spread before him, and his head sank on his breast. " We are lost ! " he said mournfully, " the whole of France has come against us."

And this mighty fleet they looked at was only a part of the whole, for messengers came to Toussaint, telling him that General Leclerc was sending one division to Port-au-Prince in the west, and one to the city of San Domingo in the south, and himself had sailed for Cape François in the north.

"My brave General Christophe is holding Cape François," said Toussaint to Raoul. "He will not allow the French to land without my authority. If I get there in time I may be able to treat with General Leclerc and avoid bloodshed." So once again they mounted on the fine thoroughbred stallions which Toussaint always kept stationed throughout the island, and again they took to the steep and difficult paths that led over the mountains and through the jungle, and again they heard the drums beating, now one side, now another, now far, now near, beating, beating, and each night men deserted and went to join the witch-doctors, and Toussaint's face grew grimmer, and he crossed himself and prayed to God and the Virgin.

They rode hard, but blood had been shed already by General Rochambeau, who landed his men on the beach at Fort Dauphin, and when the negroes came running down to the shore to see these brightly dressed strangers more nearly, he massacred them till the sands were black with their bodies, and not one escaped alive save the man who limped away to tell the tale.

In the high mountains above where the cape thrusts into the northern sea, Toussaint joined with Christophe, who told him of the fall of the city of Cape François, looking askance at the white men in Toussaint's train as he did so. Christophe was a great brutal-looking black man, but he carried his head like a king, and the glance of his eye was proud and fierce as an eagle's. Raoul told the Captain and Jacky what he said, and this was the story of it all. Leclerc had demanded Christophe's surrender, and when it was refused, then the Frenchman sent a proclamation of Boney's, which set forth that if the blacks did not submit, the indignation of the French Republic would devour them even as a fire devoured their dry canes. Next morning, Leclerc had landed his men at a point to the westward, and Christophe, knowing that the new town of Cape François, built on the ruins of the old, could not be defended, set fire to it, to its gorgeous palaces lined with rare woods, and retreated to the hills with his followers, leaving the smoking ruins to the French.

Now began a strange life indeed in the steamy jungles of the interior. Toussaint and Christophe planned out their campaign, sending letters to the other black generals in other parts of the island, and the French general sent letters to Toussaint trying to get him to give in and give no more trouble. Leclerc made many fair promises to Toussaint and said he would make him chief of all the island under himself, but Raoul urged the black man not to believe any of this. " I was in Paris, I heard it all," said Raoul : " the First Consul swore he would destroy you and bring the country under the heel of the masters once again. They are telling you lies."

Jacky didn't like those days in the mountains ; the jungle was hot and dank, and even the flowers and the creepers looked strange and devilish, and always at night the drums beat like a pulse through the thick woods, yet they never could come upon either the drums or the drummers. Even Captain Lovel, whom Jacky had never seen frightened, hated the drums, and would sit close to Jacky by the fire, and talk to him, looking now and then over his shoulder at the blackness of the forest. "Those are the witch-doctors' drums," he said, " and I don't like them ; they know too much about queer things, these niggers. I wish to God we were away and running before the Trade."

Captain Lovel talked to Jacky a good bit, which he had never done before, but then he too seemed lost in a queer sort of way : Jacky wondered whether it was being on shore instead of at sea that made the Captain so different from his confident self ; and yet, somehow, there seemed to be more than that in the matter. Once Jacky over- heard the Captain and Raoul quarrelling, or at least not quite quarrelling, but speaking oddly to each other.

" I came here to please you," Jacky heard the Captain say to Raoul, " and to get this mule-headed nigger away. He won't come, so it 's no damn good hanging on here. I don't know what is happening to my vessel. I have got to get back, and you must come with me."

" My friend, I owe you many thanks," said Raoul in that polite way of his he never lost. " You have indeed sacrificed a great deal for me. If you feel you must go, I cannot stop you, but I must stay here."

" You want to go back to Ennery to see that bread-and-butter Yankee girl, I suppose," said the Captain in a rage, and then Raoul was in a rage too, and it made him very white and still. He didn't answer, only turned on his heel and left the Captain, and afterwards Jacky saw Lovel follow him and put his hand on his arm and say something, and presently they shook hands. But from that day, Raoul never seemed as friendly with the Captain as he had been. It was to Jacky that he spoke of his sorrow. He could not fight for Toussaint and against his own countrymen, neither did he like to desert the black man and the cause of liberty. But the Captain was very angry, and reminded Raoul of his parole, and ordered him to come back to the *Moonraker* with him next day. But the next day something happened which altered everything. Another letter came from the French camp, and Toussaint sat with it in his hand, and his eyes filled with two tears that fell over and slipped down his black cheeks. Afterwards Raoul told Jacky what was in the letter. The French general had written him saying that his two eldest sons, who had been educated in France, were being sent to his house at Ennery, with their French tutor, and that they would be bearing a letter of peace and goodwill from Boney.

" My sons ! " said Toussaint to Raoul, " I shall see my sons. The First Consul is sending them back to me as a pledge of good faith."

They were two days riding from Ennery ; Toussaint bade farewell to Christophe, and then he and his bodyguard and the three from the *Moonraker* rode hard with only a few hours for sleep, so that it was soon after dawn on the second day that they rode down into the fertile valley, and saw again the white house amongst the palms. Every one was tired except Toussaint, and he was far ahead even of the two trumpeters who were always supposed to be just behind him. He always rode on a feather bolster placed across his saddle, and this last night he had ridden sixty miles without dismounting save to change from one fine thoroughbred stallion to another. Now as they reached the level green meadows, he set spurs to his horse and galloped far ahead. Jacky saw him draw rein before the verandah, and leap to the ground, and the same moment two youths ran out from the house. Toussaint gave a great shout and held out his arms, and the two boys were clasped to his breast ; there they stood, all three, holding each other. A pale man came out and stood on the verandah looking at them, and saying nothing.

CHAPTER IX

IN WHICH TOUSSAINT TAKES LEAVE OF HIS
FAMILY AND RAOUL REFUSES TO TAKE LEAVE
OF GONAIVES

THE pale man was Mounseer Coisnon, the French tutor, and he was a very smooth-spoken man and a liar as well, so said Raoul. Apparently he told Toussaint that Boney only wished for a peaceful revival of colonial relations with submission to the Republic. If Toussaint would agree to this, he was to go at once to Cape François and submit to General Leclerc, but if he refused, his sons were to be taken away from him and kept as hostages. The tutor laughed and joked with Raoul, for he thought a fellow Frenchman would sympathise with him. " I waited for the old man to clasp his sons in his arms," he said, " and when I had seen him shed tears, I knew that was the moment to step forward and take advantage of his softening, and give him the letter from Napoleon. I said to myself : ' Now I have him ! ' " Raoul turned his back on the other Mounseer and left him.

Madame Toussaint thought the tutor a very kind, nice gentleman, and she and both boys begged Toussaint to believe in him, and the General sat and listened with his head in his hands.

Now Placide, the eldest boy, was Madame

Toussaint's son by another man before she married
Toussaint, and Isaac was the General's own son,
but he loved them both equally, and he wished to
give them their choice whether to go with the French
or to stay with him and the blacks, whom the French
wished to betray into slavery.

Jacky, watching what took place on the verandah
from amongst the bushes in the garden, saw it all
like a play in dumb show, and his eyes pricked with
tears and his heart beat quickly, for he felt that
something terrible was happening. The tutor
joined in and seemed to be urging something, and
at last Toussaint sprang up and took his children
into his arms and kissed them, while they and his
wife tried to hang about him, and he shook his head
and turned to go. Placide sprang after him and
said something, and Toussaint seized his hands,
and then together they went into the house.

Toussaint would not see Isaac again for fear
even his strong heart might weaken, but flung himself on to his horse and called for his bodyguard.
His family stayed in the house by his orders, all but
Placide, who leapt on to a horse beside his step-
father just as Raoul, followed by Jacky, came up.
Toussaint bade them farewell, smiled once again
at Jacky, but hardly as though he saw him. Jacky
thought he was looking very determined, even
fierce, and for the first time he realised that the
General could be stern as well as just. Then
Toussaint rode away into the mountains with

Placide and his trumpeters and his band of faithful
followers. Mounseer Coisnon started away back
to the Cape, very white and angry.

Old Madame Toussaint sat on the verandah
crying quietly, and Miss Laura, looking, Jacky
thought, just like a little white angel, brought the
other children to her, and they clustered round her
and climbed into her wide lap, where they slipped
on the glossy silk ; but though she put her arms
round them, she still wept. Raoul stayed in the
garden with Jacky, and presently Captain Lovel
came out to them. His mouth was set in a thin
line, and Jacky had never seen him look so angry.

" This has got to stop," he said roughly ;
" you 've failed in your mission, you come back
with me now." Jacky thought it a great pity that
Raoul had had to give his word to go back to the
Moonraker, for, after all, she was a pirate vessel, and
now that he was free of her, he had better stay free ;
Jacky himself had every intention of getting left
behind if he could possibly manage it, for though
the island frightened him, yet he could easily pick
up another vessel there. Raoul seemed to hesitate
for a minute, and then the Captain flashed out :
" What about your word of honour ? You will
break that, I suppose, now it suits you ! Didn't
you promise me that if I risked hanging for myself
and capture for my vessel, and brought you here,
you would leave again with me whether you had
succeeded or failed ? "

" I am not trying to get out of my promise," says Raoul, holding his head very high ; " those were your terms, and I accepted them, but I don't agree that my mission has failed ; he will want us yet."

" I will give you twenty-four hours more," says the Captain, " and not another minute." And with that he turned as though to walk off, and then changed his mind and came back and suggested that they should ride down to the sea at Gonaives, and take one of the fishing-boats drawn up there on the shore and prospect along the coast in a southerly direction for a bit. " For," said he, " we will go back to Port-au-Prince by water, and I would like to choose the best and most hidden cove where we can hide if we have to."

Raoul didn't seem to want to go very much, but there was no denying the plan was a good one, and for the rest of the day they sailed back and forth, past the high cliffs and the jewel-green slopes that ran down to the sparkling beaches. And they found deep natural harbours where ships of the line could have sheltered, yet Captain Lovel would keep on sailing, so they did not get back till nightfall.

That night everything seemed changed suddenly in the house amid the palm-trees. The pomp and stateliness were still there, but seemed suddenly to be empty glitter ; there was a feeling of disaster abroad. Madame Toussaint ate little at dinner, and went on crying gently ; only the American ladies kept up a pretence of everything being as usual, and Raoul helped them with talk about Philadelphia. He could not talk of Paris.

Miss Laura was a little grave, but she was lovely in rose-colour, and Jacky couldn't take his eyes off her from the far end of the table, where he sat humbly by himself. After dinner, she sang and played the harp. Jacky had never seen any one so pretty or so kind. She even tried to make friends with Captain Lovel, who hardly answered her, and yet seemed unable to take his burning eyes from off her. Jacky wondered if he too was sweet on her, the same as Mounseer Raoul was, but had a different way of showing it.

CHAPTER X

THE twenty-four hours lengthened into two days and nights, and always Raoul begged for more time, and always Captain Lovel cursed and gave in. Then on the third day there came a nigger messenger out of the jungle, galloping on a jaded stallion, and his face was grey with perspiration and with fear. He carried with him a printed proclamation that had been issued by Leclerc, which said that General Toussaint and General Christophe were to be " without the protection of the law." All citizens were ordered to pursue them and to treat them as enemies of the French Republic. When the blacks on the estate had the notice read to them, they broke out into a great wailing, and nearly all ran away into the forests.

" Hell's bells ! " said Captain Lovel, " this is the finish ; the French may get my vessel, for they 'll be swarming round Port-au-Prince before you can say knife, or draw one, either. I 'm going back to my ship, and you, Raoul, are coming too."

Jacky could see that Raoul was very miserable, but he had to stand by his word if Captain Lovel insisted, and he hadn't even the excuse that he wished to fight beside his countrymen, for though he wouldn't fight against them he wouldn't fight on their side either. " Do you insist on my redeeming my word and coming back with you ? " asked Raoul, standing up very straight and pale, and Captain Lovel answered and said : " By God, and by Noah, who was His first admiral, I do."

" Have you any objection, then," said Raoul, " to saving the lives of the white women by taking them aboard your vessel ? " Then there was a moment's silence, and then Captain Lovel made answer : " I 'll take them if they want to come, but I won't answer for it saving their lives ; they 'll be much safer with the French. My ship is not a nursery. She flies the Jolly Roger and not a baby's bib."

Raoul flushed up and turned and went into the house, for he and the Captain had been talking on the verandah. Jacky never knew what Mrs. Pounsell and Miss Laura said to young Raoul, except that they refused to leave Madame Toussaint. They were very pale, both these ladies, but very brave. Raoul came out again in a great state of despair, and he took Captain Lovel away into a corner of the garden and talked with him a long time. At last the Captain agreed that, anyway for a month, they would stay as he had intended, off the island of Tortuga, which lay north of Gonaives. The *Moonraker* could lie in one of the bays of the smaller island, and the men be kept contented with fishing, and hunting for treasure, and perhaps an occasional brush with the French. If General Toussaint changed his mind, he could escape thither and come aboard.

" You and I, Raoul," said Captain Lovel, " will start at once.   You can't stay here to fight against your own kith and kin, nor yet against the man who saved your life when you were a youngster."

" I am at your service," replied Raoul, with a little bow ; but it seemed to Jacky that his heart was sick.

" As to you, boy," said Captain Lovel to Jacky, " get yourself ready.   We start to sail in an hour's time."

" Ay, ay, sir ! " said Jacky, saluting. And he tied his things up in a bundle, kissed Toussaint's little girls good-bye, made his bow to the ladies, and then carried his master's valise down to the fishing-boat. He stowed the load aboard in the stern-sheets, and then went back up to the house. There he met Raoul coming quickly down the steps from the verandah, and he saw the whisk of a peach-coloured gown as it fled into the house.

" Jacky," said Mounseer Raoul, " are you coming with us, back to that pirate ship ? " and Jacky stared at the young Frenchy and said : " Yes, sir, I suppose so."

" Why do you come, Jacky ?   You have given

no word of honour ; why don't you stay free and honest ? "

" I 'd like to, sir," said Jacky, " but what am I to do if I stay here ? If the Frenchies don't kill me, the blacks will."

" My friend General Toussaint, who has never broken his word or betrayed a trust, will look after you, Jacky. Go to him, and be a friend to him if you can. Bring him to us if he will only come."

Jacky thought for a moment till his mind seemed to go dizzy, wondering what he had better do ; he was grateful in a way to Captain Lovel, who had always treated him kindly, if you forget that he might have been the death of him in the first place ; he was even in a way fond of him, for the Captain seemed to depend on him somehow, and to like having him near him ; yet he wanted to break away from the pirate ship, for if they were caught he might be hanged along with the rest of them, and a bullet through the heart in a good fight was a better way of ending his life, if it had to end, which he very much hoped wouldn't be for many years to come. And he liked Mounseer Raoul far better than he liked the Captain, better than he liked any one in the world, for he seemed almost as young as himself, and he was brave and honourable and simple, and though Captain Lovel was brave enough, you couldn't say that he was either of the other two things.

As to General Toussaint, he made Jacky feel

uncomfortable. He was, in a queer sort of way, although only a poor blacky, something like a god. A queer sort of human, unhappy god, who would get more unhappy and probably be beaten, and yet be finer than any one who beat him. In short, he was strange, and although Jacky admired him, he couldn't quite feel he liked him. Jacky's own eyes had smarted with tears, and his throat had ached when he watched that dumb show on the verandah, and yet he had been angry because of the tears that had run down Toussaint's cheeks. An Englishman wouldn't have cried, not like that, quite simply, as though he weren't ashamed of it. It was unfair that a black man could make you feel everything that this General Toussaint made you feel.

Then, as Jacky stood hesitating, suddenly there seemed to swim up in the golden air before him that sad black face with the mournful eyes, and they were watching him, and he shut his own for a moment, so that his lids became like sea-shells against a flame, over his eyeballs. They shut out the sad dark eyes of the black man, and for a moment he seemed only to be listening to some strange little voice within his own heart, and he opened his eyes again and said, " I will go with the General, sir."

Raoul shook him by the hand and pressed on him all the money he had in his pockets. " Listen ! " said Raoul, " you must escape up into the woods now, and lie there till evening. I will send the messenger who brought the proclamation after you, and he will take you to the General. Don't forget, Jacky, tell him he can't fight against France. He will be crushed. Try and bring him to us in Tortuga."

" But I shan't be able to come back to the ship if I desert," said Jacky.

" I 'll make it all right with the Captain, Jacky," answered Raoul ; " I think I can. I 'll get word to you somehow when I know where you are. Leave it to me. You see, Jacky, I gave my word to Captain Lovel to go back to the ship with him, but I promised him nothing after that. I shall consider myself free once I have kept my word to return with him. I may join you, Jacky, or I may think it my duty to find Miss Laura and Mrs. Pounsell and look after them. Let us make Miss Laura our post-office, Jacky. I will send her letters for you, and you do likewise if you can. Toussaint will be sending messengers ; give him your letters."

So Jacky promised, and then he got on a horse, and a servant filled a water-bottle for him and slung a great bunch of bananas and a bundle of bread over the saddle, and Jacky rode off, hidden by the thick green vegetation that grew along the side of the meadows. Sitting on his horse an hour later, half-way up the mountain slope, he could hear the blast of the Captain's whistle blown again and again, more and more impatiently, from the beach, and he grinned a little all to himself. Something not going all your own way for once, my fine fellow, thought Jacky; and he peeled and ate a banana.

CHAPTER XI

NOW Jacky lived a strange life for many weeks,
fighting in the mountains and in the valleys
along with Toussaint l'Ouverture. He began to
think that he might never see Captain Lovel and
Mounseer Raoul again. He seemed to himself to
be living in a dream which had become real ; a
dream of hot damp greenness and bivouac fires at
night, of black faces that glistened in the light of
the flames, of strange sickly-sweet smells and
sudden alarms ; a dream of blood and pain and
killing, and of sleep heavy as death. General
Toussaint kept him always by his person, but there
was no need to protect him, for the blacks, when
not frightened and angry, were a merry, childlike
folk, who loved dance and song, and often indulged
in both for his amusement before the campaign
grew too hard. Jacky learned a funny French,
short and clipped as the blacks spoke it, and in a
way he quite enjoyed himself.

He soon saw that Toussaint was not quite the
sort of man Raoul thought he was—he was stronger,
he could be ruthless as well as merciful ; he kept
strict discipline. One day two men who had
murdered a planter were brought to him, and he
had them shot out of hand. He had, Jacky found

E

out, relentlessly put down all opposition when he
made himself master of the island, and during his
rule he had made the people work, though for the
first time it was for fair wages. He was a master
of men.

Jacky also began to see what a good general the
black was. The French had grouped themselves
in three divisions, with the object of all meeting
together at Gonaives, so as to capture Toussaint's
family and take possession of his headquarters ;
but Toussaint was setting ambushes and harrying
the enemy, and prevented them from surrounding
his troops or from joining together into one over-
whelming army. Rochambeau, the general who
had murdered the blacks on his first landing, was
in the mountains above Lacroix, to which place
Toussaint had had his family conveyed. Rochambeau was anxious to get there, so that he could
capture Madame Toussaint, and at the same time
cut Toussaint off from connection with the great
black general, Dessalines ; but to arrive at Lacroix,
Rochambeau had to pass through a deep gorge
where the flanks of the mountains were dense with
forests. Toussaint filled these forests with armed
labourers, who had flocked to his standard ; he
felled trees and closed the defile with them. The
French came pouring into the gorge, and all day
long the battle raged. Toussaint himself, at the
head of fifteen hundred of his picked grenadiers,
four hundred dragoons, and over a thousand

infantrymen, led the battle against the Frenchmen, and both sides fought hand to hand all day long in the blazing heat with great gallantry, and at last each side had to retire, neither vanquished, only utterly spent, but Toussaint had stopped the French advance and saved his family. General Toussaint would not let Jacky charge with himself and his men, but kept him in the rear, where Jacky had to content himself with bringing up ammunition and taking water to the wounded. At first Jacky was disappointed because of this, but by the end of the day his heart was sick at the dead and dying men and the dead and dying horses, and he went into the forest and lay down under a great silk-cotton tree, between its tall roots, and laid his face against the moss that was wet with dew and tried to forget it all, and thought he never would, and then, suddenly, he was asleep.

After that it was all skirmishing backwards and forwards over mountains and through forests so dense that the black soldiers had to cut their way with their machetes. Toussaint knew he could not defeat the well-armed thousands of the French in open battle, so his method was to offer resistance at every point, and when he had to retire, to leave fire and desolation behind him.

In the middle of March Leclerc issued a proclamation giving back the cultivators to their old owners, and the terrified blacks, the dread of slavery in their hearts, came from all over the island to join Toussaint. Even the planters themselves thought it too soon for such a measure, and that it would be unsafe for them to return to their estates ; and the blacks who had gone over to the side of the French at once began to desert into the woods. Every day more and more rallied under Toussaint and he swept through the country at the head of a large army, driving the French back into Cape François. It is true, most of the soldiers were only armed with machetes or with cocomacaque clubs, but they were all angry now, and frightened at the thought of further slavery.

One day, soon after the battle in the ravine, the great black General Dessalines arrived at Toussaint's camp, and Jacky saw him face to face. This man was different indeed from Toussaint or from Christophe. Toussaint was small and toothless but dignified, and there was something that glowed from behind his black face which no one who saw and could understand ever forgot. Christophe was hard and austere, cold and deadly, and a great man too. Dessalines was great, but it was a greatness that was for himself. Toussaint stood for liberty, Christophe for power based on liberty, but Dessalines for power based on bloodshed. He had a great frame and always wore a coat, to hide, so awed negroes whispered to Jacky, the scars of flogging inflicted by white men, but his face was cut into strange and terrifying patterns by the tribe to which he had belonged when as a little boy he had been stolen from the coasts of Africa. He gave one look at Jacky, cold and venomous, brushing past him with his tall black body and huge shoulders as though Jacky were a small white lamb that he spurned from his path. He was followed by a man who looked white, but whom Jacky found was a man with negro blood called Lamartinière, with a gallant bearing and dark earnest eyes. A pretty young mulatto girl had her arm through his. She carried a gun over her shoulder, and a machete hung from her belt. Black silken ringlets fell on her shoulders from beneath the red cap of Liberty perched upon her head. Neither she nor Lamartinière noticed Jacky; they were looking into each other's eyes.

For a long time Jacky heard the low deep rumble of Toussaint's voice, and Dessalines' and Lamartinière's answering it. Presently the strangers vanished into the blackness of the night, but word of them came back again and yet again to Toussaint's camp. Dessalines and Lamartinière had been sent to hold the post of Crête-à-Pierrot; they held it strongly and well, that bleak, parched, rock-bound place, where the heat quivered like a wind-flaw on water, but where everything was dry and barren.

The pretty mulatto girl fought like a man, and she fetched and carried ammunition, and the precious drops of water which grew less and less. When food, ammunition, and water were at an end, Dessalines set fire to Crête-à-Pierrot, and he and

his remaining seven hundred men fought their way
out, and got away in the night. They left to the
French a barren city wrecked by bombardment
and by fire.

All this time Toussaint was everywhere in turn.
He harried Leclerc in the rear. He went from
Gonaives to Marmalade, from there to Plaisance.
Dessalines murdered every white man, woman,
and child upon whom he could lay hands ; the
white men slaughtered all the blacks, down to the
smallest piccaninny. No one was buried, for there
was no time to dig graves, and blacks and whites
were for ever coming upon the bodies of their own
people or those of the enemy lying tumbled by the
wayside, half-eaten by the wild dogs or vultures,
or, on the banks of the rivers, by crocodiles.

" Ah, Jacky ! " said Toussaint, one night by the
camp fire, " if there were only one white nation
that would support the cause of freedom ! France,
England, America, all are slave-holders. I alone
fight for freedom."

" Mounseer Raoul is all for freedom, sir," said
Jacky. Toussaint smiled, but though his smile
was kind, it was a little sad.

" It is true he loves Liberty," he said ; " she is
a goddess he admires. But we are not fighting for
an ideal, Jacky ; we are fighting for the actual
liberty of our bodies, that they shall not be ill-used."

CHAPTER XII

CHRISTOPHE was fighting in the north, Dessalines in the west, and Toussaint moved from one to the other, supporting each in turn, till the French, worn out by the heat and the strange foods and by disease, never knew on which side he would strike. There were blacks fighting on the side of the French, men who believed in Leclerc's promises of freedom, and mulattoes who wished to rank with the whites. There were whites fighting on the side of Toussaint, men who cared for the cause of freedom, and men who had held plantations and traded freely in the prosperous and peaceful days of Toussaint's rule. No man knew who was his friend or foe, no man knew what to believe, no man knew where he would be next day, or whether he would be alive or dead.

A feeling of gloom again spread through the black army, and again the throbbing of the Voo-doo drums began to echo through the forests, and Toussaint grew more and more grim.

Jacky asked Toussaint one evening what the drums meant, and why they should make him sad. " They make me sad," said Toussaint, " because they mean my people are slipping backwards. They are not trusting to our Lord and His Mother.

Don't seek to look into these things, Jacky, they are of the devil."

He asked one or two of the soldiers to tell him what the drums meant, but though they would generally chatter away about anything they would say very little now. One man said that he could not tell him what went on for fear of the Papalois and Mamalois, and when Jacky asked what these were, he explained that they were the High Priests and Priestesses, and that the words meant " Papa Kings " and " Mamma Kings."

Another man told Jacky he must not ask about things that concerned the Sacred Snake, and suddenly Jacky remembered the green snake he had tried to kill at Jacmel, and how the people had prevented him.

Jacky became more and more curious, and night after night he lay awake listening to the drums that seemed now near, now far, but always calling, calling, calling. One night, when the moon was so bright that even in the depths of the forest you could see the shapes of the tree trunks quite clearly, Jacky saw two men get up and begin to steal away through the undergrowth, going so cautiously on their bare feet that hardly a leaf rustled. Perhaps, thought Jacky to himself, if I follow them I shall be able to see the witch dances. And he, too, got cautiously to his feet and began to creep after the others, and though he made more noise than they did, nobody awoke.

Jacky followed the men for so far that he began almost to wish himself back at the camp fire. He was afraid he might get lost and never find his way back, and he had heard many strange and terrifying tales from the blacks about what happened if you got lost in the jungle at night ; evil spirits caught you and never let you go, and your body and soul would both be lost to all eternity. However, he knew he might never get back by himself, and so he kept on after the two soldiers, though it sometimes seemed to him they must be going the wrong way, for the drum often sounded farther off, but always after this it suddenly burst out again, apparently quite close at hand. Then it grew fainter and fainter, till Jacky could hardly hear it at all, and yet at that moment he came upon a clearing in the jungle, and there before him, only about thirty yards away, the drummer was beating on his drum.

The drum was very long, and the drummer sat with it between his knees, and he was playing on it with his fingers, thumbs, and palms. He went on and on, quite monotonously. His head was thrown back, and his eyes were rolled upwards, his shoulders swayed, and his whole body swayed as he drummed. Jacky didn't break through into the clearing ; he was afraid of what might happen to him if he were seen. His heart was beating thickly, and he crouched back behind the leaves, so that his white face and hands should not show in the moonlight. He stayed very quiet, and gradually his eyes grew accustomed to the patterning of light and shade that the moonlight had made over the clearing. A great fire burned in the centre, and its leaping flames added to the confusion of the shadows, making them seem alive. About fifty or sixty men and women, nearly naked, were standing in the shadow of the trees round the edge of the clearing ; they beat their hands softly together and swayed from side to side. Beyond the fire a couple of goats were tethered, and they, unlike the humans, were clothed. Somehow Jacky thought that that was the most frightening thing that he saw ; those goats in their ill-cut jackets and trousers, with their bearded faces and lewd yellow eyes moving restlessly in the firelight. A bundle of cocks lay on the ground all tied together by their legs. Jacky could hear their faint squawks, and he saw that they were both white and black, and that they were decked out with bits of coloured rag. Jacky saw the two soldiers that he had followed helping themselves from a great puncheon of rum which stood beside the drummer. Then every one burst into a low song, a sort of chant like you might hear in church, but it didn't sound very like church music, for all the time some of the blacks clapped their hands, and others swung calabashes filled with little stones back and forth, so that the air was noisy with their rattling.

Now the drum began to go faster and faster,

and the dancers moved their feet and their whole bodies faster and faster in time with it. The two soldiers that Jacky had followed came out into the clearing ; and an old woman in a scarlet wrapper came swaying out into the firelight and stood before them jerking her body this way and that. All the people sank on to their haunches and bowed their heads as though in worship. Their shoulders still moved, but their feet were still. An old man with a sort of crown on his head brought forward one of the cocks and handed it to the woman, and she whirled it round and round her head by its neck so that its white feathers flew out and floated lightly down upon her great black arms and shoulders. The next moment she had thrust the bird to her mouth and torn off its head with her teeth. Jacky had seen hundreds of fowls killed, and had himself killed a good many, yet now he felt deadly sick, and had to hold on to the trunk of a tree for fear he fell down, his legs were so weak under him. The Mamaloi ran round and round screaming, while the blood dripped from her lips, and a few white feathers clung to them. She stepped down and smeared the bloody neck of the cock over the faces of the two soldiers, and gave them each to drink from it as though it had been a flagon. All the men and women began to jerk themselves upwards from their haunches till they were standing erect, and then they poured in a great black tide, still dancing, up to the fire, and began to dance

round it, enclosing the Mamaloi and the Papaloi ;
and the two soldiers, mouths slobbered with blood,
danced in the ring that they made. Jacky could
see no more except a glimpse now and then. Quite
close by him several of the dancers fell out and
lay rolling on the ground locked in each other's
arms. The acrid smell of sweat reeked in his
nostrils. He heard the high whinny of a goat as
some one laid hands on it, and he caught one fleet-
ing glimpse of a frightened bearded animal face
above a torn coat-collar, then he saw a black body
bend over it and caught the gleam of an upraised
knife, and he turned and ran back into the jungle,
not knowing where he was going, but only sure that
he must get away ; that no evil spirits in the jungle
could be worse than the things round the fire.

He crashed through the undergrowth, making
a noise that sent his heart to his mouth, but those
he left behind him were too absorbed by now to
notice any sight or sound from without their
charmed circle. Jacky stumbled on and on through
the jungle, climbing always upwards, for he knew
that he had gone downhill when he followed the
soldiers ; and just as he was thinking in despair
that he must have gone in a circle and be coming
back to the fire, so loud was the drumming, he found
himself back at the outskirts of the camp. He had
been very lucky, he knew, and he fell down in his
old place, with his head pillowed on his bundle,
which somehow looked to him so oddly innocent

because it was lying just where he had left it. He lay and shuddered, and sleep would not visit his eyelids, across which passed in endless procession dancing black figures, and blood that fell in jets like water blown from a fountain.

He wished he were back on board the *Moonraker*. Stained as were her decks, and with the blood of honest men, yet they were clean somehow compared with this blood that he had seen spilled and drunken in the depth of the jungle. They are worse than beasts, thought Jacky miserably ; why am I with them ?

The next morning he avoided Toussaint and all those blacks who had been his friends. He took his stew of Congo beans and went to the far end of the camp, where he could be quiet and alone. He was startled to come on two very old blacks, a man asleep, and a woman alert and watchful, who were seated beside a great heap that lay along the ground. He bent forward to see what it was, and to his horror saw it was a young girl and a youth, both white, lying asleep under a cloak. They were so alike that they must be brother and sister. Jacky turned to run and tell Toussaint ; the blacks must have brought these two, drugged, to sacrifice them, like in the stories he had heard now and again in the island. Surely Toussaint would try and save them. . . . But he no longer felt sure even of this.

He found Toussaint at his elbow, and started with alarm. But the General was smiling down at the little group of black and white people beneath the tree.

"There had been a massacre of the whites, alas!" said Toussaint, speaking softly, "but these two faithful servants saved their master's children and brought them through the jungle and over the mountains to safety with me. They have had no rest or food themselves, for they had given all to these whites and watched while they slept. Now they have eaten, but see, the old nurse still will not sleep. She watches to see that no harm can come near."

The old woman must have thought that Toussaint's voice would waken her charges, for she held up a warning finger to him, frowning a little, while the old man stirred uneasily in his sleep. Toussaint nodded and smiled, and walked away with Jacky.

CHAPTER XIII

ONE day news was brought to Toussaint from
the north coast, and Jacky saw him sitting
with his face buried in his hands, and he found it
was because General Christophe had made a treaty
with the enemy and surrendered. Leclerc had
promised Christophe that his rank should be re-
spected, and that he should keep his authority under
the French Government.

In a proclamation, Leclerc said that it had been
impossible for him when he arrived in San Domingo
to understand the nature of its people as he now
did, and that now he promised liberty and equality
to all. But he added that, of course, this could not
be definite until it had been approved by the French
Government. Christophe had then joined the
French and now held rank under them. Dessalines
had next made his peace, and Toussaint was left alone.

General Leclerc began writing letters to Toussaint, and the black general made the best terms
he could for his people. Leclerc promised him
their freedom, and that he himself would be treated
as a valued friend and citizen of France. And so
Toussaint rode to Cape François to give up his
sword. All the way the country people crowded
to see Toussaint pass, weeping and blessing him,

and begging him never to desert them and the
cause of freedom.　Jacky and the other white youth
and his sister were with him, and they rode on
into the ruined town, where the blackened stone
houses were powdered over with white dust, and
the great glaring spaces were sun-baked and weary
in spite of the strong breath of the north-east wind,
which brought fresh life to Jacky after the weeks in
the jungle.　They came to a sort of temple in the
middle of the square, and some one told Jacky that
this temple had been built by the blacks in memory
of their having been freed from slavery.　It had
steps all round it, and a great dome with seven
pillars under it, and within the pillars two seats,
and between the seats was a pole with a cap of
Liberty at the top of it.　Toussaint stood looking
at this for a moment or two, and his big lips moved
as he read an inscription that there was, all about
freedom, over to himself.

General Leclerc was awaiting Toussaint in his
palace by the sea.　He was a little pale man, sickly
looking, with anxious eyes.　By his side was a
woman so beautiful that when he saw her, Jacky
forgot Miss Laura, whom he had thought the
prettiest girl in the world.　She was dressed more
like one of the heathen goddesses that you saw in
beauty albums than a real lady ; and her neck and
arms and bosom and her sandalled feet were white
like a statue.　She was Boney's sister Pauline,
wife of General Leclerc.

She tittered when she saw the shabby little black
general in his stained and ragged uniform, and
held up a plumed fan before her lovely face. Toussaint paid no heed to her, and General Leclerc
bowed and spoke very politely. When it was all
over, and the French general had again promised
the black general freedom for himself and his
people, there came a little stir from the group of
ladies and officers in the background. A young
girl came forward and put both her white hands into
the hard black palms of the vanquished black man.
It was Miss Laura, and Jacky felt his heart lighten
for the first time for many a day.

CHAPTER XIV

IN WHICH JACKY RECEIVES TWO LETTERS

MISS LAURA nodded and smiled at Jacky, and later a message came to him from her. He had gone with Toussaint to the Hôtel de la République, which had been the pride of the city, indeed of the whole island, before the burning. It was still a fine shell of a place, though the gorgeous polished woods were cracked and blackened, and the many-coloured marbles stained with smoke.

"Dear Jacky," wrote Miss Laura, "I send you a letter that I have been keeping for you. A certain gentleman has not seen fit to honour us with his presence at Cape François, save the once that he conveyed us hither, neither has he written me fully of his news or his friends. I am staying here a while with Madame Leclerc, and then Mrs. Pounsell and I will be taking ship for Philadelphia. Should you not find a vessel to suit you before then, I will be glad to speak to the Captain on your behalf. I should not like to think of your having to go back to a vessel under the command of such a villainous fellow as Captain Lovel. At your age good influences are of the utmost importance.— Your friend and well-wisher,

"L. Delamere."

" *P.S.*—Should there be any news of importance in the letter which I have enclosed to you,
perhaps you will come down to the Palace to-
night. I shall be walking on the terrace at nine
of the clock."

Jacky read this letter through quickly, for he was
anxious to tear open the one that he knew must be
from Mounseer Raoul. He was so excited that for
a moment or two he could hardly make out the
writing, though it was very plain and clear.

" MON PETIT JACKY," wrote Mounseer Raoul,
" At last I have got news of you ; I hear you did
very well in a battle, taking water to the wounded
of both sides, and that you did not heed the
bullets flying around you. I have much news
to tell you, but I shall be brief, for I expect soon
to see you. Things came to a strange pass with
me on board the *Moonraker*, but that I am not
free to tell you of yet awhile. I accompanied
the Captain back according to my promise. We
stood out in the fishing-boat round the western
end of the island of Gonave, so as to avoid the
shipping anchored off Port-au-Prince, and we
found the *Moonraker* still lying undiscovered
in the cove where we had left her. There was
some rioting and discontent among the men,
for they had had too little to do, and were tired
of chasing wild pig. Red Lear was full of

grumbles and ill-pleased to see me back, as you may guess. The Captain soon established law and order again, and indeed, for discipline commend me to this law-breaking vessel. The second night on board I had a talk with the Captain, and told him that having returned with him, I now considered myself free of my parole. I had made up my mind to return to Ennery as soon as might be, in case Madame Toussaint and the American ladies needed help and protection. The Captain saw that my mind was made up, and short of putting me in irons, he could not prevent my escape. However, this thing became known to me, of which I cannot tell you in a letter. The Captain told me something which in a certain measure binds me to a greater chivalry and gratitude than otherwise I should have deemed needful. Had it not been for this, I should have considered the account between us settled. So at length we came to an agreement. I was to sail with him to Tortuga, but there I was to be free to go to and fro as I pleased. We sailed the following morning, and are now lying in a well-hidden creek off this island of the buccaneers. The men are contented again, and the hunt for treasure goes on. They have found a few pieces of eight, which has increased their enthusiasm. I have twice sailed myself in a small boat to the Cape, but have kept away as much as possible from my fellow countrymen. The first time I received news that the household at Ennery was to be removed up into the mountains, and I was able to make arrangements to transport the American ladies to the care of Madame Leclerc at the Cape.

" I got news of you, *mon petit ami*, from the blacks who acted as their escort as far as Esther, where I met them. Miss Laura's good heart made her grieve at leaving Madame Toussaint.

" I rejoined the *Moonraker* according to the arrangement I had made. I have little hope of this campaign turning out well for either side, and it may yet mean, with a neutral vessel at my disposal—for such was the Captain's vastly generous offer—that I can save both the Toussaint family and the American ladies, should any of the things I dread come to pass. The blacks may get the upper hand, when there will be a general massacre of the whites, which Toussaint would be powerless to avert, or at any moment the yellow fever, which I hear is already raging in Port-au-Prince, may attack the Cape in spite of the northerly breezes. Shortly after you receive this letter I shall hope to be with you. Try and stay at the Cape until I come. I have made your peace with the Captain ; you and I must never forget that he is generosity itself. I do not know whether you have heard any news from Europe, but I expect not, living like a savage in the forests. France and England have signed a treaty of peace, so we are no longer enemies, and I can subscribe myself your friend,

"RAOUL DE KÉRANGAL."

Now these were two cheering letters for a lad that had left England friendless, and Jacky felt very pleased and proud. He admired the young Mounseer more than any one he knew except Toussaint, and after all, the General was old and ugly and black. But even now Jacky couldn't think of him as vanquished. For, after all, it had been the blacks who made their own terms. But even more than that, it was, thought Jacky, that whatever happened to Toussaint, something within himself would remain the same. Nothing could touch that, however he was treated, and somehow, though he couldn't have explained it, Jacky saw that that was what victory meant.

He went down to the terrace of the Palace that evening—the land wind was blowing as it blows all night at the Cape—and after he had waited a while, he saw the figure of Miss Laura, wrapped in a light cloak, coming towards him. Inside the Palace there were great lights in the chandeliers, and a sound of music came out and floated away over the sea. It was very different from the ruined room where Jacky had left Toussaint writing a letter to his wife by the light of one guttering candle.

Miss Laura and Jacky walked up and down the

THE *MOONRAKER*

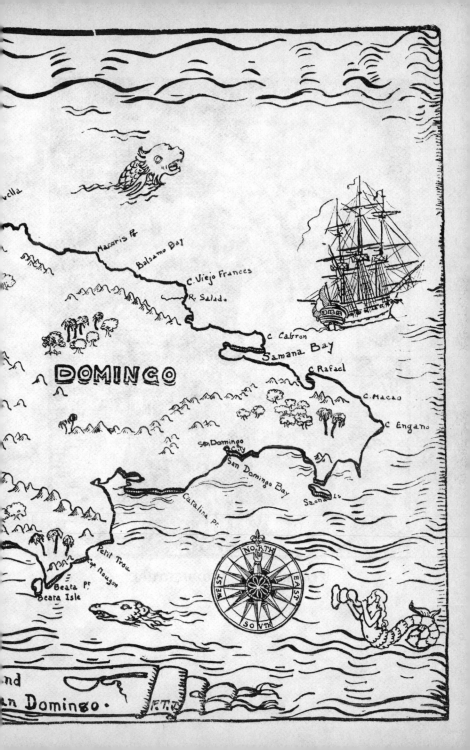

TOUSSAINT L'OUVERTURE

F

terrace, savouring the cool land breeze together.
There was something a little odd and strained
about Miss Laura, thought Jacky. Her manner
was kind as ever, but she seemed jerky and unreal,
like a doll when you pull the strings that make it
utter its little words. Yet what she said was
sensible, as everything that Miss Laura said was
sensible. She would never, like Captain Lovel, talk
of soul-ships, or such strange abstractions ; nor,
like Mounseer Raoul, talk of liberty and the rights
of humanity. Still, if she did not speak windy stuff,
she did speak common good sense, and she had
observed much.

" General Leclerc is very sick," she told Jacky ;
" he has lost heart, and soon every one will know it.
He has made mistake after mistake with the blacks
because he is afraid of Napoleon. First he tried
to enslave them according to his orders, then when
he saw that was not possible, he pretended that
that had been a mistake, but he is only waiting to
make them all slaves again."

Jacky thought of Toussaint waiting to tell his
wife that he was coming to join her again quietly
in the white house at Ennery, and his heart felt like
lead in his breast. If the old laws were brought
in again, Toussaint would be a slave ; he who had
thought himself as great as the First Consul.

" I have read the letter from Mounseer Raoul,"
said Jacky timidly, for Miss Laura hadn't mentioned the young Frenchman, and Jacky had a

feeling, he didn't know why, that she was not best pleased with him.

" Oh, have you had one ? " asked Miss Laura.

" Why, yes," said Jacky, " you sent it to me."

" Was that from him ? " said Miss Laura carelessly, " I didn't notice the writing."

" I thought you knew it was from him by what you said in your letter," said Jacky in surprise. He saw he had made a mistake, though he couldn't tell why, for Miss Laura seemed quite offended, and pulled her wrap round her and said how cold the land wind was at this time of night.

" He bids me wait here for him," Jacky went on ; " he says he hopes to come soon."

" That will be nice for you," answered Miss Laura.

" He hopes," went on Jacky, determined to say what had been in his letter, " that he will be able to take you and Mrs. Pounsell away into safety ; he fears what may happen in the Island."

" La ! " said Miss Laura, " he is too kind. He came to Esther to meet Mrs. Pounsell and myself, and I asked him then if he would not stay and afford us protection, for indeed between the odious gallantries of the French officers and the scowls of the savages, I was quite nervous ; however, he preferred to return to this Captain Lovel of his."

Now Jacky guessed that Miss Laura had no notion that Captain Lovel's vessel was a pirate, for Mounseer Raoul had considered it a point of honour not to betray this, so all he said was : " Captain Lovel has been very good to Mounseer Raoul, miss."

" Oh, indeed ! " said Miss Laura, tossing her ringlets. " But if you ask me, I imagine there is some other attraction on board. Captain Lovel has a wife perchance, or a sister. Many of these dashing captains travel with their womenfolk on board, and from the manner in which the Captain always glared at me, it seemed that he was quite nervous lest his young friend should find poor me at all attractive. Therefore I guessed it was a sister, as I imagine even Captain Lovel would hardly wish to ensure any gentleman's attention for his wife. However," she went on hurriedly, just as Jacky was about to speak, " I have no wish to inquire into the domestic arrangements of Captain Lovel's vessel. I don't know why I mentioned such a subject. Oh yes ! I remember. I was telling you I had asked my compatriot—for after all, I can count myself of French origin, although proud to be an American—to remain here, and he refused. . . . See, Jacky, there is the Southern Cross ! There is a French colonel here who has taught me where to look for it when it rises. Is it not a beautiful constellation ? "

Mrs. Pounsell then came out on to the terrace, calling to Miss Laura, and seemed shocked to find her out there so late alone, for evidently she didn't count Jacky as being anybody.

Jack went back to the hotel sadly. The next morning Toussaint mounted his horse to ride back to Ennery. The French had promised him that he could go home and live there quietly. " Perhaps, Jacky," said Toussaint, as he bade him farewell, " I shall not be unhappy ; if my people are treated well, it is all that matters, I will plough my fields and read my books. Do you know the works of Epictetus, Jacky ? " Jacky shook his head, and said he had never heard of the gentleman.

" He was a slave too," said Toussaint, " and a very good man ; I read him much. Good-bye, Jacky." He held out his hand and Jacky took it. As he stood looking up at the General on his beautiful horse, somehow there came to Jacky a moment when time seemed to stand still, and it seemed to him that this moment was going on for ever in some odd way that he couldn't explain. Always afterwards, whenever he remembered it, that moment was real as the present to him ; he saw Toussaint's ugly black face under the Napoleonic hat, where the feathers were now broken, cut out sharply against the burning blue sky. And the eyes that looked down at him were very sad.

The General had ridden off on his beautiful stallion, sitting it as though he were part of it. Whenever Toussaint was on a horse in motion, you forgot he was small and ugly, and only saw the grace and swing of him. But Jacky did not watch him out of sight, because the clouds of dust that had arisen from the spurt of the horse's heels made his eyes water, so that for a moment or two he could not see.

CHAPTER XV

THE yellow fever stalked openly through the city of the Cape. Already many had died of it and been buried secretly, but now it had become like a giant person that could no longer be hid away. Every hour messengers came in from the other towns with tales of death, and at the Cape men were afraid to close their eyes in sleep. " These are our last moments," cried the beautiful Pauline, " let us pass them in pleasure."

Every day she thought of some new amusement. She was carried through the jungle in a litter borne by sweating blacks, she bathed in a pool where the water was green as malachite, she sailed out to sea accompanied by musicians and by admirers who sang and made love to her while she trailed the tips of her white fingers in the sparkling water. The music never ceased playing at night in the Palace, though the musicians sometimes fell down writhing, and the instruments went clattering from their stricken hands. Many of the soldiers fled to the ships in the harbour, but they only took the disease with them, and the water of the harbour was filled with the corpses that were thrown overboard, so that the few ships with enough crew left to work them up-anchored and sailed away. The deserted harbour contained only hideously swollen corpses, and ships too riddled with the disease for movement. All the Cape was a great lazar-house. Jacky went to the top of the mountain and strained his eyes towards Tortuga for a sight of Mounseer Raoul coming in a little boat, or even for a sight of the *Moonraker*, which he would have welcomed, Jolly Roger and all.

Still, it would take time for news of the fever to get to Tortuga, and Jacky continued to climb the hill and keep a look-out for a dark speck on the bright waters. One morning his heart leapt to see a ship coming in under all plain sail, but as she brought up in the bay he could make out she was a French seventy-four. He went down to the harbour, and found out she was the *Héros*, from the city of San Domingo. There seemed some mystery about her arrival at the fever-stricken Cape. She had come to fulfil some special purpose, and General Leclerc was rowed off to interview her captain, and Pauline flirted with the officers on her quarter-deck, but that was all Jacky could find out.

But early in the afternoon a horseman came clattering into Cape François from the south, and drew rein at the Hôtel de la République. It was Raoul. Jacky ran out to greet him. Raoul flung himself off his horse ; he seemed very tired, and his face was ashen. The sweat was pouring off him, and Jacky saw he was trembling. " It is

nothing," said Raoul, when he saw Jacky's anxious
look. " I am only exhausted. And sick at heart,"
he added. He looked indeed like a man who had
seen a ghost, and Jacky called for a glass of rum
as he led Raoul into the hotel. He took him to his
own room, where there was still enough roof left'
to make it shady, and Raoul sank on to the low
bed.

" What is the matter ? " asked Jacky, when Raoul
had drunk the rum.

" Treachery is the matter ; a base betrayal of
faith. The Corsican has covered my nation with
dishonour." Raoul held his clenched fists against
his eyes and sat rigid and soundless. It was as
though you could hear his spirit groaning. Jacky
did not like to speak. There was something so
dreadful about his friend's whole aspect. Suddenly Raoul took his fists away from his eyes and
looked up. " I warned him, Jacky," he said. " I
warned Toussaint, but in the confidence of his
own honour he could not believe me. Who would
have thought, indeed, that a Frenchman could for-
swear himself so basely as Leclerc has done ? I
knew he would, for I knew those were his orders
before ever he left France—to take prisoner Toussaint and Christophe and Dessalines. But those
two have gone over to the victor's side. They are
working for Leclerc ; they are his useful tools.
Only Toussaint, the pure, the unbribable, would
not sell his own people and work for the oppressor.

Why could they not leave him alone ?   Jacky, he
was living so serenely there at Ennery.   I hired a
boat and sailed round to Gonaives from Tortuga,
and then I rode up to Ennery and found him.   It
was a lovely calm evening, Jacky.   Everywhere
there was peace.   He had come in from working
in the fields.   There were five or six notable people,
two of them white, from different parts of the Island,
come to him for advice.   Every day some came to
him.   Always he counselled peace.   Why should
they not leave him alone ? "

Raoul sprang up and began to pace the room.
" I will tell you why," he answered himself.   " It
is because the vanity of the Corsican will not allow
this black man to rest in peace after he had defied
him.   It is not enough for the First Consul that
he has destroyed the prosperity of the Island.   That
rivers of the most gallant French blood have been
poured out on this soil in an unjust fight.   It is
not enough that thousands of these blacks, who had
at last begun to be prosperous and self-respecting,
have been plunged back into the depths out of which
they have climbed.   No, none of this is enough
unless he can punish the man who saved the
black race from destruction and slavery, and
who has shown that he can draw up a con-
stitution and plan a campaign as well as a white
man."

" Oh, sir ! " said Jacky, " what have they done ?
Have they killed him ? "

G

" Not yet, but what can it be but a question of time ? I was there that evening with him, Jacky. All was happy and quiet. The children were playing, and I sat listening. Suddenly there comes a messenger from General Brunet. He brought a letter to him. There was treachery in every line, but neither Toussaint nor Placide could believe it. Brunet begged him to come over and see him at once at his headquarters, the plantation of Georges, between Ennery and Gonaives. The letter was very friendly. It was too friendly, Jacky. The General said he would have come himself, but he had been too overwhelmed with business. He said—I think, Jacky, some of the lies are cut into my soul—he said : ' You will find the frankness of an honourable man, who desires nothing but the happiness of the colony and your own happiness.' He said that he would like to make the acquaintance of Madame Toussaint, and would send his own horses for her. He ended : ' Never, General, will you find a more sincere friend than myself. With confidence in the Captain-General and friendliness towards all under him, you will enjoy tranquillity.' A vile letter, Jacky. What man of honour needs to make assurances that he is honourable ? Toussaint went, Jacky. He asked me to stay behind with his wife and children. Why did I do so ? But alas ! I could have done nothing had I gone with him."

" What happened ? " asked Jacky. " What did they do ? "

" They captured him in the trap that they had laid," said Raoul. ". He met Brunet at Georges. There were twenty officers there, who came into the room with drawn swords and pistols in their hands. Toussaint drew his sabre, for he thought they had come to murder him, but their leader assured him they were not there to assassinate him, but merely to secure his person, and Toussaint put his sword back in its scabbard. I waited all night for his return, and in the morning, as soon as it was light, I rode down to the plantation Georges, where I heard everything that had happened. They had already taken Toussaint under armed escort down to Gonaives, and had embarked him on the French frigate, the *Créole*. I rode back as hard as I could go, to Ennery, and there I found three or four hundred French soldiers in possession, and the blacks in a terrible state of alarm and confusion. Several of those were lying dead, for the French had fired on them as they ran panic-stricken. Madame Toussaint and her children were carried off, amidst the sobs and wails of the servants. I rode with them. They are being brought to the Cape, but I was able to go faster than they, and so I have come on ahead to see if I cannot do something with Leclerc." Jacky thought of the pinched little yellow-faced man who had received Toussaint's sword, and his heart sank. He would not say anything to discourage Raoul, only busied himself bringing water and towels, and then watched while his friend bathed himself and rearranged as best he could his disordered dress. Then Raoul went off to the Palace by the sea.

CHAPTER XVI

THAT evening, an evening clear and golden
as a bell, the frigate *Créole* came to rest in
the harbour of the Cape. She floated in like a
swan, her stunsails set, the light of the declining
sun striking athwart her starboard rail, the water
hardly ruffling from her cut-water, the image of
beauty and of peace. Raoul called Jacky, and they
hurried down to the port in time to see a small
boat being rowed from the *Créole* to the *Héros*.
They themselves went straight to the seventy-four,
and arrived at her tall and terrifying flank soon
after those from the little boat had climbed on deck.
Raoul called out something in the pure French
that Jacky found it a little difficult to follow, and a
young officer, who was leaning over the high bul-
wark, and who seemed to know Raoul, called to
him to come up. Raoul and Jacky went up to the
deck of the *Héros*.

Toussaint was standing there, unbound, but
with an armed guard on either side of him. He
still wore the uniform he had donned in which to
pay his respects to General Brunet, but the plumed
hat was missing, his greying hair was uncovered to
the soft evening air. He was very quiet and still,
only his eyes rolled in his wrinkled black face.

He looked more than ever like a sick monkey, and yet he seemed so dignified, more dignified than his spruce captors, who all talked excitedly around him. He stood quite simply, not striking an attitude, not drawn up proudly, looking sad and puzzled and rather surprised, like a hurt child. He seemed very small on that great slope of deck, with the huge trunk of the mizzen-mast at his back.

When he saw Raoul his face lighted up, and when he caught sight of Jacky behind him he smiled, and somehow that smile looked as though it were his first for many hours. Jacky tried to smile back, but his throat felt dry and tight, and he couldn't quite manage it.

The commander of the *Créole* was speaking, and Raoul and Jacky did not go forward to Toussaint, but stayed quietly. The commander of the *Héros* seemed annoyed by what the commander of the *Créole* was saying. Later, Raoul told Jacky that the French officers from the *Créole* protested at what they had to do, and that they expressed their respect for Toussaint and their indignation at the treacherous trick Brunet had played on him. The commander of the *Héros*, who confined Toussaint in a small dark cabin, and loaded him with chains, after rose higher in the service than he of the *Créole*, who had protested.

The officers of the *Créole* took their departure, and they saluted the captive black general before they went over the side. Then Raoul obtained leave to speak to Toussaint, though an officer hovered near to hear what was said.

" I will compose a letter to the First Consul," Toussaint assured his friends ; " he will see that I have a fair trial, that I am allowed to plead my cause and that of my people, when I have arrived in the mother country. But meanwhile, get our friends, Miss Laura and Mrs. Pounsell, away. I fear there may be terrible doings when my people find out how I have been treated." Raoul nodded, but said nothing, and suddenly Jacky made a diversion by calling out : " Here are Madame Toussaint and the children. They are coming aboard."

And indeed a small boat was approaching with the ample form of old Madame Toussaint overflowing the sternsheets, the children clustered about her, like a great bunch of black grapes. They all climbed up, and then every one stood back a pace, even the guard, as Toussaint clasped his wife in his arms. Old Madame wept quietly, while the children howled more loudly and plucked at her skirts.

Jacky stared out to sea, and was glad that the swift dark was falling. Already the gold had gone from rail and spar, and from a limpid blue the water had turned to a dark and sullen green. The Commander rapped out an order, and Jacky knew the time had come to go. Raoul spoke in a low voice, rapidly, to Toussaint.

" Freedom ! " said Toussaint, out loud, " freedom is a tree that cannot be destroyed. They have only cut down the trunk "—and here Toussaint stuck out his chest—" but new branches will spring up, for the roots are deep in the heart of man." And Toussaint slipped his hand within his coat after the manner of the First Consul, and stood thus a moment, before he suddenly seemed to realise what he was doing, and took his hand out again. Raoul wrung the hand in farewell, and next he bade farewell to old Madame, patting her on the back and trying vainly to console her. Then Jacky felt his own hand taken, and through the dusk he saw Toussaint's eyes looking into his. And they were so sad he turned his own away, and hardly seeing where he went, followed Raoul over the side to their own boat.

CHAPTER XVII

IN WHICH JACKY CHARTERS A
" MAMAN-PREND-DEUIL "

RAOUL strode ashore like a madman, refusing to speak even to Jacky. When they had reached the water front, striding very fast, he turned for one last look at the *Héros*. Her sails were shaken out to catch the land wind, across the water came the clank-clank of the pawls as the anchor came up, and the cries of the sailors.

Then Raoul spoke. " This is the end," he said, " this is the end. The Corsican has broken his word, and taken prisoner the man who has never been known to break his. God of liberty and justice, where were You that You allowed such things to be ? "

" He said—the General—that he would write to Boney. He said he 'd get fair play over in France," said Jacky consolingly. But Raoul only groaned.

" He will get his death in France," he said, " and the First Consul will never see him. Let us go, Jacky ; this air is polluted." And he began to stride away at a great pace.

" Yes, sir. Where are we going, sir ? " asked Jacky, and Raoul paused.

" Where ? " he asked. " Why, to the Palace, of course, to take away Laura. There is nothing

else left to do. No man could save Toussaint in
the face of his own trust, but I can at least get her
away from this hot-bed of moral and material
corruption ! "

Jacky admired the way Mounseer Raoul always
talked like a book. He trotted after him along
the water front. Suddenly Raoul stopped.

" Good heavens ! " he cried, " we have no
vessel. Jacky, you know this place well ; do you
think you can hire a craft of some kind ?   A fishing
smack ?   Anything that can take us to Tortuga ? "

" To Tortuga ? " asked Jacky stupidly.

" Yes, yes, to the *Moonraker*. She is awaiting
me there."

" There 's very few craft left," said Jacky ; " the
blackies have nearly all fled. But I can try. Along
the bay there may still be some sloop to be had if
you can pay for it."

" I have money. Promise them what they want.
Tell them to be at the steps at midnight. That
will give even ladies time to prepare, and yet not
long enough to change their minds. Here," and
Raoul thrust a purse into Jacky's hand, " take that
with you, but do not show it to them all at once."

Jacky couldn't help wondering how Mounseer
Raoul, gifted as he was, would persuade Miss Laura
to go with him, for she had seemed so very cold
when she had talked of him a few nights previously,
and as for Captain Lovel, him she detested. However, that was not his business, and he went off

through the soft blue night, where the dance of the fireflies was weaving and glittering in the depths of the air.

Jacky, after much searching and bargaining, managed to hire what the natives call a *maman-prend-deuil*, which meant, he knew, " mother goes into mourning." All the little sloops were called that, because when the menfolk of a family set out to sea in one, the mother of the family at once went into mourning, for she never expected to see them again. But there was nothing else to be had, and though it was not very suitable for ladies, there being no cabin or shelter of any kind, Jacky could only hope for the best. The passage to Tortuga should not be long, for though beset with reefs and sandbanks the negro skippers could feel their way about blindfold.

At midnight Jacky had got his little boat—she was only fifteen tons, with an open hold filled with great lumps of granite as ballast—at the harbour steps. He expected Raoul to make his appearance alone, and as time went on, he became more and more sure that such would be the case. However, half an hour after the appointed time, the cloaked and hooded figures of Miss Laura and Mrs. Pounsell, preceded by a servant carrying a dim and bobbing lantern, loomed along the quay, one on Raoul's either arm. Two black servants followed, staggering under great trunks, which surprised Jacky somewhat.

The trunks were stowed on top of the ballast, mattresses procured by Raoul were placed along what would be the weather side of the deck, and the ladies were helped on board. Now, besides her black captain, who was her owner, and her crew, the *maman-prend-deuil* carried a black pig and a black dog. The dog burst into a storm of snarling and barking, baring its teeth, and shaking itself sideways across the deck in its rage, but the skipper quieted it by a kick. Jacky explained to the ladies that these sloops always carried a pig and a dog ; the dog to guard the vessel when the crew were in the rum-shop, and the pig to eat, if, as sometimes happened, the sloop was becalmed at sea for a few weeks. Miss Laura cried out in horror.

Raoul helped the ladies to arrange themselves comfortably upon one of the mattresses, drawing up a coverlet over them, and then beckoned to Jacky to come and join him upon the other. But late as it was, and wearing as the events of the day had been, Jacky had no wish for sleep yet. His heart was aching for Toussaint, betrayed and lost, yet he could not but be aware of a leaping sensation of excitement. He felt that this was his own vessel, as none had ever yet been. He had found her and chartered her, he had given the orders. He was the leader of the expedition, and he never forgot, even when he was an old man, that moment when the mainsail rose slowly, blotting out the stars.

The little craft drew away before the light land breeze, and the water began to talk past her side. The moon rose and flooded the sea with glory, dimming the bright shining of the low white stars, and the moon-glade came up to the little sloop and went along with her.

CHAPTER XVIII

BEFORE the land wind, which freshened as they got farther out, they ran northwards, past the sandbanks and reefs to starboard. The little craft sailed sweetly along, through the deep channel past Fort St. Joseph and Le Grand Mouton. They then stood out to sea to avoid the coral reefs that lay thickly to port, and the little boat ran up and down the swell of the waves with a motion that caused the ladies much discomfort.

As the night wore on, their discomfort increased. The wind still freshening, caused more sea as they got from under the lee of the land, and as the skipper brought her up to steer more westerly, she lay over in the choppy sea, shipping it green over her weather rail so that the mattresses and those that lay upon them were wetted through and through. At first the cold and freshness was not ungrateful after the blistering heat of shore, but so soon does the human frame forget the rigour of its sensations, that it was not long before the ladies were longing to be too hot once more. Jacky came and joined Mounseer Raoul on his mattress, and they pulled the rug well over them and presently fell asleep. A loud scream woke them both suddenly.

" What 's the matter ? " cried Raoul.

" The pig ! The pig ! " cried Miss Laura in the same breath as Mrs. Pounsell cried, " The dog ! The dog ! " There, plainly visible in the moonlight, pressed against the ladies, were the ship's pig and dog ; cold and wet and frightened, they had forgotten their distrust of humanity, and had crept gently up, one on each side of the mattress, and pressed against the ladies for warmth. The negro captain lifted his foot and sent the pig spinning across the wet and slippery deck, but Jacky cried out and stopped him before he could treat the dog likewise. The dog, too, was driven away, but more gently, and the ladies settled down again. Jacky was just dropping off to sleep when he felt something very sharp and pointed sticking into his side. It was the hoof of the little pig, that had crawled back again. It crept higher and higher up him on its sharp little pointed hooves, and presently snuggled down against his shoulder. He put one arm round it and the other round the shivering dog, which crawled up his other side and lay between him and Raoul, and then they all four slept through the night in as much comfort as might be. With dawn the wind fell again and died. There were the shores of Tortuga, green and lovely as the coast of Paradise and as unapproachable. The sea lay all about them like a shield of silvery gold, and at first the ladies were very pleased to be able to shake out their skirts and get dry in the warmth, but as hour after hour went by, and still there came no breath of wind, their contentment dropped and faded. Cockroaches had got into the packet of food which they had brought with them, and the white wine and water that they drank was warm and not pleasant flavoured. The sea became a shield of brass. There was no strip of shade in the tiny vessel as the sun rose overhead. By noon every one was wishing for the cold and the wet and the boisterous wind of the night. The westerly current that sets towards Tortuga Channel helped them a little, but not so that you could notice it. Then suddenly a little breeze sprang up, the sail began to fill and hope sprang high, but it was simply a catspaw, and died away again. Soon after this, however, the true wind began to blow once more, and again the boat ran before it at four knots towards the shimmering shores.

They found the *Moonraker* lying at a cable's length from the shore, under the lee of Saline Point, at the western end of the island. There she lay, as smart as paint, light as a sea-bird on the water, her canvas trimly furled. The wind had died away entirely, and her reflection went down into the sea as in a mirror. The *maman-prenddeuil*, propelled by sweeps so rotten that Jacky feared they would crack every time that the stress came upon them, looked like a water beetle crawling towards the beautiful *Moonraker*. Miss Laura and Mrs. Pounsell arranged each other's dress, somewhat disordered from the experiences of the night. Miss Laura looked very pale but very beautiful, Jacky thought. Jacky was a little nervous as to how the captain would receive him, although Raoul had promised him all would be well.

As a matter of fact, the Captain merely nodded, rather grimly, at him, for he was taken up with greeting his guests. He took Raoul's hand and held it a moment without saying anything, only giving him a look so deep and quiet, that it was, thought Jacky, the friendliest look ever seen on that lean countenance. He bowed very politely to the ladies and bade them welcome on board his poor vessel in a very polished manner. Certainly something seemed to have changed the Captain, and very much for the better. Even Miss Laura observed so much to Mrs. Pounsell when Jacky, by the Captain's orders, showed them to their stateroom. Mrs. Pounsell had always considered the Captain a very personable man, and said as much rather reprovingly. Jacky fell into his duties again in the first minutes on board. He took great pitchers of warm water to the ladies, filled glasses with rum and fresh limes, and altogether felt as though the past weeks were some strange dream. The Captain bade him help himself to a shot of the rum, and he was not slow in doing so.

Jacky tipped a barrel of potato peelings and such-like stuff on to the deck of the *maman-prend-deuil* for the pig, and gave the dog a bone, which it bore off, growling, into the bows. The captain of the sloop was paid off, and he and his crew were given drinks and some bales of scarlet cotton that Jacky recognised as having come from the *Piskie*. Sight of them gave him a strange pang at his heart. It was so long since he had given a thought to poor Billy Constant.

The sloop's sail shivered and dilated in the light breeze that had begun to blow, and slowly she drew away from the *Moonraker's* high black side. Jacky stayed staring, lost in thought, till old Red Lear's grumbling voice swore at him for a lousy lubber and a bloody soger, who was no good for anything but getting in a proper sailorman's way. Jacky went below.

CHAPTER XIX

IN WHICH JACKY TALKS WITH MOUNSEER RAOUL

LIKE a disordered and frightful dream that slips away from the mind on awaking was the island of slaves as it fell away from the swinging stern of the *Moonraker*. The white wake turned and twisted back towards the high green mountains, as the thoughts of the dreamer may still turn backwards to the perils he has braved in his sleep. The high verdant mountains dwindled to a line of misty grey, and then the greedy rim of the world swallowed them up altogether. Jacky stared till they were gone, and wondered whether Toussaint, from his place of confinement, had been able also to look his last.

Through the Windward Passage, leaving Great Inagua to starboard, through the Crooked Island Passage, sailed the *Moonraker*, so as to get north into the westerly winds as soon as might be. Jacky wondered whither they were bound. He didn't like to ask Mounseer Raoul, for the young man looked ill and haggard, years older than the talkative enthusiastic youth of a few months earlier. Jacky, too, felt changed. It was not that he was now a man, that he had been in battles by sea and battles by land, that he had suffered hardships and seen strange sights; it was that, in a little over three months, he had seen the whole of life in one man's

face, and that face a black one. For the General
had shown him—and without knowing it—high
hopes, not for his own self but for mankind ;
shown him faith and trust and love and sacrifice,
and after Jacky had watched these things he had
seen them betrayed. Had he not been captured
by the *Moonraker*, he might have followed the sea
for years and seen none of these, or lived at home
in Saltash and missed them there also, and now
that they had made the stuff of his life they lay
heavily upon his heart. So he went quietly about
his duties, and thought of Toussaint upon the
high seas.

The Captain didn't notice him. From having
been a favourite he was now in disgrace, but he did
not wonder at that. Miss Laura gave him a smile,
but though it was kind, all the life seemed to have
gone out of it, somehow. It was as though the
smart and lovely *Moonraker* were under a blight.
There was a feeling of something strange abroad
in the ship. The men themselves were discon-
tented and full of grumbles. True, they had had
two good prizes, but that was near five months
ago, and since then they had not been able even to
raid the island of San Domingo, though in the
general confusion it would have been a simple thing
for a landing-party to sack a city or so. But Captain
Lovel would not have the blacks attacked, because
of Mounseer Raoul's friendship for this General
Toussaint, who was a prisoner now anyway.

There was much coarse joking for'ard about the presence of ladies on board. Not that any one imagined the Captain was interested in the ladies ; he had never been known to show a spark of interest in a petticoat ; still, there was no denying that something had got hold of him, and when that happened to a man it was always either a woman or religion. It might have been thought that he had got religion, but he swore just as much as ever, and was never seen reading a Bible like a good Christian, or crossing himself like a black Papist. It was a bad business altogether. Here he was, almost the last successful pirate in the North Atlantic, piling up riches for himself and his men, a splendid navigator, as bold a devil as ever trod quarter-deck, and now he was risking his vessel and all his men's lives unnecessarily, and without chance of gain, right in the track of all the men-of-war that sailed between the Bermudas and the West Indies. What the hell was he after ?

But if they grumbled about the Captain, the men treated Jacky with a new respect. They had picked up word of his doings from time to time, and several of them now tried to pump him, but Jacky had nothing to tell them.

The opinion generally held aboard was that the *Moonraker* was making for some point of land where she could disembark her passengers, and then she would be free to go her piratical ways again. This opinion was held at first with a certain com-

plaisancy. The ladies, being American, were
doubtless rich, like all that rebellious people, and
it was thought not unlikely that something well
worth having and sharing out was going to be the
reward for the waste of time and the extra risk of
taking the Windward Passage. Talking it over
together, the men decided that the Captain must
be making for one of the Bahamas. The *Moonraker* could not, of course, go into Nassau, but she
could put off her passengers at one or other of the
little islands to the west of the group—at Rum
Cay, or Concepcion Island, or Watling Island.
Coasting schooners trading in salt, sponges, turtles,
timber and the like, were always trading between
the various islands and the coast of North America.
One or two of the men on board knew these waters
well, and were full of wise remarks and good advice,
but as they could only give it to each other, it didn't
change the *Moonraker's* course.

Jacky listened to the talk when it came his way,
which it didn't do very much, for his work lay aft,
and he knew it all sounded very reasonable. And
yet, somehow, he could not help feeling that reason
was not going to enter very much into the Captain's
actions. Why he felt so sure of this he couldn't
make out. He only knew that he was.

The *Moonraker* kept on, and when she was well
through the Crooked Island Passage the wind came
away, as it is apt to do in those parts at that time of
the year, to south'rd of east, and the *Moonraker*

braced up her yards and sailed close to the wind, instead of running before it as she would have if bound for Rum Cay.

That afternoon, the third after leaving Tortuga, the look-out men gave a great shout and reported a sail. The vessel, when she drew nearer, appeared to be a Frenchman, by her lines and the cut of her sails. She was a merchantman, probably bound for South America with a rich cargo from the ports of Europe or the East.

At once the men of the *Moonraker* forgot their discontent. They were like men who have been lying becalmed when a fresh wind blows once more. Consternation, therefore, was dire when the Captain forbade the preparations for battle. At first, the men could not believe that the *Moonraker* actually meant to pass the stranger peaceably. They thought the Captain must have some cunning plan up his sleeve, but when the *Moonraker*, having shifted her helm, lay on a course that would take her astern of the Frenchman, they understood that there was indeed to be no fight. An angry deputation came into the waist of the ship, and the Captain came forward to the break of the poop and flung back curses. He held a pistol in each hand, and swore he would shoot if the men did not lay for'ard before he had counted ten. Jacky never forgot the hard beat of the Captain's voice telling the count, or the bright living venom of him as he threatened the men from above their up-

turned heads. They wavered and broke and went
for'ard, but they still muttered angrily and stood
about in groups under the fo'c'sle head with
lowering faces.

Red Lear was seen to go into the Captain's cabin,
and for a long time a low rumble of voices could
be heard, then Red Lear came out, his face redder
than ever in anger, and he went for'ard and would
speak to no one. Later Jacky came on Raoul and
the Captain talking, and Raoul was begging the
Captain to sail westerly and put them off at Watling
Island, which was still on their port beam. But
the Captain simply sat and said : " I 'm not going
to land you. I shall hold on, even if it 's to the
coast of France, and into the jaws of the British
and the French fleets rolled into one ! " Raoul
shrugged his shoulders, but he looked very angry.

The wind veered right to the southerly for a
few hours, and the *Moonraker* trimmed her yards
and steered north-east. It was obvious that she
meant to leave the Bahamas astern. Could it be,
wondered Jacky, that she was going to risk carrying
on to the Bermudas, that haunt of British men-of-
war ? Or—and this was more fantastic still—that
the Captain meant to sail Mounseer Raoul all the
way to France and risk certain capture off the
French or Spanish coasts ?

That evening Raoul called to Jacky to bring him
some wine in his cabin, and when Jacky took the
goblet in, Raoul told him to shut the door. " I

want to talk to you, Jacky," said Raoul. " My heart has been too heavy for converse or even for much thought of late, but, Jacky, I fear that we have got ourselves and the ladies out of the dangers of San Domingo only to plunge ourselves into greater difficulties. True, there is no yellow fever here, but there is another fever that may be as dangerous."

" What is that, sir ? " asked Jacky.

" It is a thing called love," said Mounseer Raoul, " but as to what it is, Jacky, that I find it difficult to say."

Jacky knew, of course, how Mounseer Raoul regarded Miss Laura. That was a thing he had always been certain of. He could not tell why it should make the young man so gloomy. He waited in silence there, for presently Raoul spoke again. " I am indeed in the devil of a quandary, Jacky," he said.

" Can I help at all, sir ? " asked Jacky, and Raoul shook his head.

" You can't do anything, Jacky, but we are friends, you and I, and that always helps a little. I wish you would talk to Miss Laura, Jacky, and cheer her up. Mrs. Pounsell is too sick to be much good to her." And in answer to Jacky's look of surprise, which said plainly, Why don't you cheer her up yourself ? he added : " It would not do if I am seen talking too much to Miss Laura."

That was it, then, thought Jacky. The Captain was in love with Miss Laura himself, though he had such an odd way of showing it, and he was jealous of Mounseer Raoul. That was why his friend said that love might be as dangerous as yellow fever. The Captain was not a man to stop at bloodshed. He had shown as much in the pursuit of what he wanted.

CHAPTER XX

THE feeling that all was not well on board the
Moonraker had grown so strong next day
that all men felt it, and each looked askance at his
neighbour, as though dreading some dire thing
might be about to befall, and wondering whence
it would come. The cook, who was a mulatto
from Jamaica, gave it as his opinion that some one
in San Domingo had put obeah on the Captain,
and the steward was told to search the cabin for
cock's feathers and bits of worsted in a bottle.
When the search failed he hinted darkly at strange
poisons, introduced in the food the Captain had
taken when on shore. He had never been the
same man since he had ridden away from Port-au-
Prince that day in January. Red Lear muttered,
" He 's never been the same man since that accursed
Frenchy came aboard."

Whatever might be the reason, it was clear that
they were laying a north-easterly course, and that
there was something unexplained, even alarming,
to simple pirates who lived by sea-robbery, at
work between the mainmast and the stern-post.

That strong life of the Captain's, that violence,
restrained but always there, by which he had held
his men, had weakened. He was silent and

119

remote, but not without a sense of deep purpose. Only the purpose no longer had anything to do with the *Moonraker's* purpose or that of her men. It had to do with these strangers he had taken aboard, with the Froggie and the American wench. That sounded simple, and yet it wasn't. None of the men was contented with the state of affairs, for although they approved of a course which would take them into the path of luckless merchantmen once more, they wished to have got rid of the passengers first. For it was darkly hinted amongst them that some one, the Captain or that young Mounseer, had decreed that there was to be no fighting while the petticoats were aboard. The *Moonraker* was a damn girls' school, and the Captain was mad. The cook must be right when he said some one had put obeah on him. Young Jacky, you've been with these damn niggers on shore all this time, and you're damn thick with the Froggie and the skipper, what do you make of it all ? By God, we won't stand it much longer. Young Jacky could say nothing. All he knew was that the young Mounseer was as anxious as any one.

As for Jacky, he felt as though, in spite of the good winds, that they were indeed all held in some charm, bewitched in some queer calm place, dangerous as the quiet heart of the cyclone, where no winds blow, and where strange creatures of leaf and wing, so say the sailormen, crowd together and hang unnaturally in the still air. From one side or another, or from several at once, the violent gusts would come that would perhaps cripple them, perhaps blow them all into yet another and stranger space, the space called Eternity. No man could say what was the strange feeling that was in all their hearts, yet every man was aware of it, and uneasy to the core of his soul.

The happiest person on board was Mrs. Pounsell, who had recovered from her sickness, and had a great admiration for the Captain, and she was always covering him with motherly attentions. She now produced some knitting and set to work to make him a hug-me-tight, much to the smothered mirth of the men.

They had left the Bahamas well astern, when one morning, Miss Laura, who was sitting in her cabin, opened the door and called to Jacky to come in, and he entered, cap in hand.

" Jacky," she said, speaking low and quickly, her breast rising in her agitation, and her grey eyes fixed upon him, " I am frightened. I know now what this ship is. At first I was too ignorant, but I wondered at all the guns, more, surely, than any merchantman would carry. Then I talked to that fierce man, Red Lear they call him. He hates us all, Jacky, but he hates Raoul the worst, and he seems to think I may be the means of taking him away for ever from the *Moonraker*, and so he talked to me. Jacky, I wish I had the power to leave this

dreadful ship and take him with me.   Do you know,
can you find out, whither we are bound ?   Are we
to sail on for ever in this manner, as though we
were on board the Flying Dutchman ?   The few
days I have been in this vessel seem to me years,
I would far rather have risked yellow fever and
perhaps massacre in San Domingo than been
imprisoned in this ship, at the mercy of this dreadful Captain, whose very glance fills me with
terror. . . ."

" The Captain wouldn't hurt you, miss," said
Jacky, in surprise. " He 's sweet on you."   She
stared at him.   " What did you say ? "   She began
to laugh a little.   " O Jacky, but he hates me.
Hates me so that he would like to see me dead.
But tell me, do you know whither we are bound ? "

Jacky shook his head.   " We all thought to put
you off on one of the Bahama Cays, miss. We
think now she 's bound for the Bermudas ; she 's
laying a course for them.   But doesn't Mounseer
Raoul know ? "

" I don't know how much he knows. I don't
know . . ."   She wailed the last words.   " He
won't tell me."

Jacky was very surprised at this, and, as always
when in doubt, he said nothing at all.   Miss Laura
wiped her eyes with a little handkerchief, and
smiled at Jacky.

" Don't tell any one I asked you, Jacky.   Especially the Captain."   Jacky gave the promise, and

as Miss Laura seemed to have nothing else to say, he carried her wraps up on deck for her and made her comfortable on the poop. Red Lear was near by, and gave them a sour glance. Presently Raoul came on deck. He came straight over to Miss Laura and sat down beside her, and began talking to her, a thing he had not done before. Red Lear gave a grim smile. The brilliant blue sky and sea was overcast by a thin grey haze, as though one looked through smoked glass, the very foam seemed tinged with a livid yellowish cast. The *Moonraker* fled on, a high thin wailing in her shrouds. The Captain came on deck and saw the couple talking low and earnestly under the lee of the rail. A red colour ran up into his lean cheeks ; he called to the young Frenchman to come and speak with him. Raoul said, over his shoulder, " I am speaking with this lady," and did not move. Jacky, at the head of the companion, the evening rum glasses in his hands, held his breath. Red Lear stared ahead, his cheek bulged by his quid.

Captain Lovel walked over to Mounseer Raoul and spoke again, in a thin hard voice.

" I command on my own quarter-deck, mister. By God, I 'll have you put in irons if you disobey me."

" You employ the wrong weapons to take a man captive," said Raoul. " They are all you have at your command, I presume."

There was a moment of silence so profound

that even the noises of the vessel's way seemed to have ceased. Then the Captain turned on his heel and came towards the break of the poop. Jacky saw he was walking like a man stricken by blindness, his blue eyes wide and staring, but seeing nothing. Jacky drew aside, and the Captain passed him by and went into the chart-house.

CHAPTER XXI

JACKY thought there was going to be trouble, and he was therefore surprised when the Captain, an hour later, told him to bid the guests to a dinner with him that evening in the stern cabin, and bade him make special preparations. The Captain spoke from the cabin he slept in since the arrival of the ladies, over his shoulder to Jacky; his voice sounded much as usual, and he was busy, Jacky saw, turning out a chest. Piles of rich silks, and a Cashmere shawl, were half poured out of the chest. Jacky stepped forward and asked if he could help, but the Captain told him sharply to get out, and Jacky went.

Evidently it was to be a festival for the crew as well as for the afterguard ; a cask of rum was sent for'ard and a whole side of pork. Jacky was bidden to set the table with the fine old silver stolen several years before from a Spanish vessel. There was much loot in the *Moonraker* that Jacky had never yet seen, things such as those silken garments in the chest, that the Captain had stored away by him for some reason, instead of selling them, or taking them home to his womenkind. But then, as far as any one knew, the Captain had no folks, no spot whither he could repair in safety and take

I

his ease on shore. Other men might desert, or
when they had made their pile, go home to spend
it in the odour of respectability, but never either
Captain Lovel or Red Lear. They were men above
taking their ease, and they took their pleasure in
the exercise of their chosen profession. Only when
chasing and fighting did the Captain's eye light up,
and the strong colour leap on his high cheek-bone.

Jacky, setting his silver, thought idly over these
things, as often before, and thought what a strange
being the Captain was, how hidden in his thoughts
and swift in his actions, how violent and yet how
quiet, with the quietness of an animal that waits
and waits. Jacky always knew more or less what
other people would do ; Toussaint, black as he
was, had acted like a man, and a finer man than
any you would meet, thought Jacky. Once you
knew him you knew what he would do, more or
less. Mounseer Raoul now, he was a Frenchy,
and yet you knew what he would do. It might
be something rather highfalutin', because that was
his nature, but at least you could make a guess
at what it would be. Red Lear would growl and
curse at every one but the Captain. As for Miss
Laura, she might be haughty, though never with
Jacky, only with Mounseer Raoul, because he was
sweet on her, and that was a thing females always
took advantage of, but otherwise she was just as
sweet as new milk. Only the Captain had always
been queer from the beginning.

At first Jacky hadn't noticed it ; it was so strange to be on board a pirate vessel that it seemed natural every one on board should be strange too. Then the men had begun to seem just like any other men to him, which had been very upsetting to his notions of good and evil. Still, he had got used to that, but the Captain had never seemed to get like other men, and although he had changed from the man he had been, no one could say quite what he had been before or what he was now. Through everything he stayed unknown ; all you could say was that now you knew still less what he was after or how he would turn. This dinner now, what did he mean by it ?

Raoul was the first to enter the stern cabin. He was dressed with his usual care, in fresh linen and a fine broadcloth coat. He was pale and very grave. Next the two ladies came in, Mrs. Pounsell still wan, but recovered from her sea-sickness, in her grey silk, looking a very proper gentlewoman. Miss Laura, for the first time, seemed the girl Jacky had seen that day in the little white house at Ennery. She wore the peach-coloured gown, very scanty and limp, as ladies' dresses were in those days, and girdled beneath her little breasts. Her hair was dressed high, and shone like a burnished helmet. Her cheek was pure and fresh, her eye bright and serene. She met Raoul's look as he hastened forward to meet her with one such as she had not given him for long past. Her little jealousies, her coldness, all were gone since Raoul had spoken to her and to the Captain on the poop.

The Captain's voice was heard shouting for Jacky, and he hurried to the cabin door. A moment later he returned with the message that the Captain was unavoidably delayed, and begged them to begin without him, and to drink of the old Canary that he had had specially broken out for them. After a polite demur they settled themselves at the table, and Jacky poured the wine and handed round the dish of prepared alligator pears. The hanging lanterns shone brightly, and the world beyond the ports looked blue and dense against the panes. No one spoke much ; it was as though the very air held a sense of waiting for something.

In the silence, that was not broken but only marked more clearly by the slap and swish of the racing sea past the ship's side, and the creaking of her framework, the latch of the door suddenly made a sharp noise. Jacky sprang to open it, and swung it wide. And there, the dark alleyway behind her, and the lights of the cabin shining full upon her wide silk skirts, stood a woman. Like a ship in full sail, rather than like any of the scantily clad women Jacky had seen in his life, she stood there, her breast rising sharply, and a creaking sound coming from the region of her waist.

Raoul had risen, checking the exclamation on his lips. The ladies sat, speechless and staring. Jacky, staring also, felt some memory that had always nagged at him slip into place in his mind. He saw again the reddened face and throat, the white shoulders, the hard proud glance that he had seen in the troubled water at old Tamsin True's. The Captain brushed past him, and came into the full light, head held high. The stiff old-fashioned silk, a yellowy white, made a noise like the rustling of waves past the ship's side.

CHAPTER XXII

IN WHICH JACKY FILLS THE CAPTAIN'S
WINEGLASS

RAOUL was the first to move. His face was flooded with colour, and he stood up and bowed low. Then he drew out the chair at the head of the table and stood waiting beside it. The Captain bowed awkwardly to the assembled company, and then settled the full skirts in the chair. Miss Laura gave a sort of little choking sound, half a sob and half a giggle. Raoul pushed forward the chair under the old-fashioned ballooning skirts, bowed gravely, and went back to his own place. Now that the light shone fully on the Captain, Jacky, though no arbiter of the modes, could see how strange a figure this was in the stiff and stately gown. Jacky's brain felt excited and yet clear. So much that had always puzzled him had now fallen into place, helped by his memory of what he had seen in the bowl of water at the cottage on the moor. This must be what Raoul had meant when he wrote that the Captain had told him something which altered everything, this must be why he had told Jacky they must both always remember what they owed to the Captain. To Jacky, brought up on tales of pirates, who knew all about Anne Bonney and Mary Read, the truth was clear as crystal. Therefore it was with

130

surprise that he heard Mrs. Pounsell's prim tones.

"Dear me, a masquerade, Captain! Vastly amusing, I am sure, but I think Mr. de Kérangal would have made the more likely-looking lady. Or our young friend Jacky; he could dress up as a very pretty girl. Your countenance is too truly manly."

"You are mistaken, madame," began Raoul, but the Captain interrupted him somewhat loudly.

"Not at all; you show great discrimination, ma'am. You think it is a good joke, but might have been a better if carried out by either of the handsomer young men. What is your opinion, Raoul?"

Raoul studied the Captain gravely for a moment. "I think it is a pity," he said slowly, "but that, of course, is your own affair. I do not assume the right to criticise your actions."

"Perhaps this is to show you otherwise. That more is changed than my garb," said the Captain in a lower voice than hitherto.

"I have no right," repeated Raoul.

Miss Laura had been sitting watching with bright eyes, silent. Now she spoke.

"The Captain has done quite rightly," she said. "He has taken the best way to show us what a fine man he is by showing what a poor sort of woman he would have made. How did you know, Captain Lovel, just how that white silk would show up the sunburnt manliness of your complexion, that is so becoming to one of your sex, and so fatal to a woman who hoped to aspire to charm! And that mode of gown! So old as to seem positively outlandish! I suppose our grandmothers wore dresses of that fashion!"

"I got this gown out of a French merchantman ten years ago," said the Captain, speaking in a queer slow way, and moving uneasily from side to side a head unaccustomed to the pearls that bound it.

"When I was a little girl in the nursery!" said Miss Laura. "There has surely never been such a complete change in fashions as in these last few years. You have certainly shown us, Captain Lovel, how foolish those women called 'blue-stockings' are, who think to ape the male, by showing us how unbecoming 'tis to the male to ape the woman!"

"What do I lack?" asked the Captain, more loudly. "This gown may be out of the mode, but it is good silk and finely embroidered. My skin has never known a blemish, my shoulders are white. My eyes are blue, which I have been told is considered a beauty in a woman. There is no white in my hair."

"Oh, Captain!" cried Mrs. Pounsell, "Miss Delamere meant merely that your gifts were unfitted to a woman, not that they were not a rich dower in a man, and man is, after all, the noblest work of God. But a woman, Captain! You know, I feel sure, as well as any of your sex, what is admirable in a woman. Gentleness, fragility, meekness. Even, if I may so express myself, a pleasing feebleness. You would hardly wish to lay claim to any of these qualities, and they would ill become you."

"Yes, that is just what I meant," said Miss Laura. "As to your eyes, Captain, indeed, they are both blue and bold, and in a lady the latter quality destroys the charm of the first. There is no white in your hair, but how much more than a mere brown hue is needful to make her hair a woman's crowning glory! Gloss, skilful tiring. . . . It is admirable the way you have managed to scrape your queue up on to the top of your head in the semblance of a knot, though I could wish you had called Mrs. Pounsell to help you. Why, Captain! . . . what is that creaking noise? La! I do believe you have forced yourself into stays! That is true devotion! What is your waist? A good thirty inches, I dare guess. Ma'am, has not the Captain indeed worked hard and sacrificed himself to provide us with a little laughter? Do we not make a pretty pair of sisters?"

And Miss Laura slipped from her chair and came and knelt by the Captain's, so that her gleaming hair, her fresh young cheek, her innocent grey eyes, came next that weather-beaten countenance. What the two ladies had said laughingly was seen to be indeed true.   The Captain had been a person-able young man enough, but as a woman was too rough-hewn, too compounded of carven wood and coarse tints. The lines made by years of screwing up the eyes and staring out to sea, the harshness of skin brought about by salt and sun, the square shoulders and flat lithe form that had made a hand-some figure of a young man, made an unattractive spinster of thirty—that vast age. Miss Laura's face looked like a flower beside that set visage.

"Raoul," said the Captain, " you have not given us your full and true opinion on my masquerade. Tell me, do you think that years of bloodshed, of dangers, of everything that goes to make the life of such a man as I, for ever sets him apart ? Is not what is handsome in him handsome in a woman ? Health and strength and courage, are these things of no avail except in a man ? Must a woman have a waist distorted out of all semblance to nature, have a timorous disposition, a squeamish sensibility ? "

"A man likes to think he can protect a woman against any need for timorousness," said Raoul. The Captain laughed.

"I know what men consider the chief thing in a woman," he said. "Chastity. Well, virtue need not always go with a smooth face, Raoul. Women have lived strange and hard lives and been as chaste as snow."

"I do not doubt it, believe me," said Raoul.

" Every virtue save kindliness could belong to such a woman. She need have no vice save cruelty. But that destroys her."

" Cruelty ! " said the Captain, with a little laugh. " Cruelty ! " And he flicked the smooth cheek of Miss Laura, still pressed against his shoulder. The cheek flushed a little, and Miss Laura sprang up and went back to her place.

Mrs. Pounsell looked bewildered, and took a protesting sip from her glass of Canary wine. Jacky was standing with the wine in his hand, as he had stayed ever since the Captain's entry. Now, he did not quite know why, he stepped forward and filled the Captain's glass. Their eyes met for a moment. There was something terrible behind the hard brightness of the Captain's.

Don't mind—don't mind ! Jacky wanted to say ; they 're not worth it. You 're the finest devil of a woman that ever trod shoe-leather ! But he couldn't say it aloud. All he could do was to fill the rummer to the brim. The Captain gave a little nod, and picked up the glass and drained it. Miss Laura gave a high little laugh. " The Captain certainly does not drink like a lady ! " she said.

" Laura," said Raoul, speaking very low and deadly, in a tone he had never used to her before, " it ill becomes you to forget, whatever our host does, you owe him gratitude and respect." Laura turned crimson.

"You take her part against me!" she cried, her eyes filling with tears. Raoul stared at her. "You know!" he said. And "You have told her!" spoke the Captain, as pale now as the sunburnt skin would permit.

"I have never broken my word," answered Raoul. "What you confided to me has been kept in confidence." Miss Laura began to sob. "You knew and never told me! How unkind! I see it all—you could not resist this—this swashbuckling lady"—her little mouth fairly spat out the unaccustomed word—"that is why you always refused to leave this hateful ship."

"I shall certainly go mad," observed Mrs. Pounsell in a resigned voice. "Do I understand that this is really a—a female, after all?"

"Of course it is!" answered Laura. "I knew it soon after we came on board. That horrid old man called Red Lear told me."

The Captain bounded up, face crimson. "Red Lear to betray me! Red Lear! Ah, that's what comes of having women on board! Boy, go quickly and fetch Red Lear to me!" Jacky hastily left the cabin, only to run into Red Lear crouching outside the door.

CHAPTER XXIII

IN WHICH JACKY LISTENS TO THE CAPTAIN
AND RED LEAR

NOW Jacky had grown big and strong during his campaigning, and Red Lear was a spidery sort of man. Jacky, very wrathful at this eavesdropping, seized him by the collar and kicked him into the cabin. Red Lear picked himself up and stood looking round him, then his eyes fixed themselves on the Captain's face.

"I knew it!" said Red Lear. "I knew you were working up for foolishness. Twenty years of hard sense on the high seas and the infernal woman not dead in you yet. I thought I'd learned you better, but there's no getting rid of original sin. By God and the devil, but you look a fine fool standing there like a stuck pig, Captain Lovel. Or shall I call you Sophy? Pretty Sophy Lovel. You look like a drab, a Dolly Mops at a fair."

"What I am you made me," said the Captain sombrely.

"I made you a man, and you throw it all away for this yard of pump water that calls itself one."

"This," said the Captain, motioning to Red Lear and speaking to Raoul, "is my father. He used to follow the sea, and then he got religion and married my mother and settled down as a preacher, Bodmin way. My mother couldn't stand him or his preaching, and she left him for a travelling showman when I was seven years old."

"She was a devil, like all women," said Red Lear. "That's why I took you to sea and reared you as a boy. Didn't I do my best by you? Didn't I thrash it into you that no one must ever know your shameful secret? And you kept it well enough till this young whey-face comes in your path. And when you got on so fine, and showed what a genius you were with a vessel, and that you didn't give a brass farthing for any puling notions of right or wrong, wasn't I proud when you were voted captain of the first vessel we took in a fight? Haven't I served under you as faithful and obedient as though I wasn't your father at all? A great name and a great fortune you were making for yourself, and now look at you! Trying to be something you can't ever be, for you can't, and don't you make any mistake about it. Why, take a look in the glass, my poor Sophy. Oh, I heard the young lady making a mock of you, and I don't wonder at it. I told her what you were to make her fiery jealous, so 's she 'd get her fancy man out of this ship and leave you be. A figure of fun you look alongside of she!"

Sophy Lovel sat very still. The dash and fire that had made Captain Lovel what he was, had gone out of her. She was a haggard woman, awkward in her body, badly dressed. She raised her eyes and looked round the cabin.

" Have I indeed been such a fool, Raoul ? " she said. " I had no notion it was such hard work to be a woman. This dress—it is of good silk. I had always kept it because it was so white and rich, like a bride's dress. It seems it is but a dowdy thing, and a woman would look better in a shift than dressed in it. As to my looks, I could often have had all the girls in port after me, if I had so chosen. It seems that as a woman my looks are not so good. I have never wanted a thing I could not get. I thought my man's garb unpleasing to you, after I had told you my secret. I thought that dressed like this you would see me anew. I have been thought much of for my courage and address ; do these count against me ? Are they any reason why I should not be a loving mistress ? I could have given you a soft bed, and riches, and a fine ship, and the life best worth living in the whole world." She rose and kicked away the chair from behind her, and drew away from the table so that she showed her whole length against the dark panelling. No one spoke, and suddenly she took hold of the top of her low bodice in both hands and wrenched at it, tearing it asunder. Her bosom, white as foam, small and delicate as that of a young girl, was exposed.

" You used to thrash me to teach me to keep my shameful secret," she cried to Red Lear in a loud voice. " Here is my secret, one no longer. Plunge your knife in and have done with it."

That was Sophy Lovel's only moment of beauty, but beautiful she was for the space of a few heart-beats. It was not possible in that place to look at any one else.

Raoul turned away and put his hand over his eyes, it was as though something had struck at him. Even Red Lear shrank back, his fierce rage fallen on shame. For a half minute Sophy's fire sustained her, then she seemed to crumple. She fell back against the bulkhead, and began to try and pull the torn bodice together across her breast. " My coat," she said, " bring me my coat. I am too ugly for such gear as this."

It was Laura who ran forward, Laura who put her arms about her. " Don't mind, my dear, don't mind," said Laura. " Forgive me. It was only that you didn't know how to do it ; you are truly handsome, I could show you how to be hand-some." She turned and stamped her foot at the men. " Go away, all of you, cannot you see she does not want you ? "

They were holding to each other, those two, when there came the noise of trampling feet from the deck overhead. Then the mate's voice raised above the shouting of the other men. A shot rang out, followed by a cry, and the thud of a body falling on the deck.

" By God, it 's mutiny," cried Red Lear. " I warned you of this when you refused to chase that Frenchman."

The Captain seized pistol and cutlass from a stand of arms, and heedless of all but the urgency of the moment, rushed from the cabin, Red Lear and Raoul hard on her heels, but Jacky, who had been standing by the door, was before them, and had already leaped up the companion that gave on to the quarter-deck.

CHAPTER XXIV

NOW there were two ways on deck from the stern cabin. One was by the alleyway and out by the door opening beneath the break of the poop, and the other was by the companion that led directly from the cabin door to just aft of the wheel. It was up this companion that Jacky had leaped, and the first thing he saw was the body of the mate sprawling face downwards on the moonlit deck. The blood that had trickled from under it looked like a skein of black yarn against the white planking. Half a dozen of the mutineers were on the poop. The carpenter, a huge figure of a man, came charging across the deck at sight of Jacky, but Jacky fired, and a dark patch appeared on the man's white shirt-sleeve ; he checked a moment and then came on, flourishing his cutlass, looking very huge as he reeled along.

It was at that moment, like some strange and nightmare-like Jack-in-the-box, that Captain Sophy sprang up from the dark square of the hatch. As she leaped forward into the moonlight, with her dishevelled hair and shining cutlass, the swelling surfaces of her skirt caught and held the light so that she seemed to flicker with it like some moony apparition risen from the waves. The men fell

142

back as from a ghost, stricken by the strangeness of what they saw. She charged down the deck straight upon the giant carpenter, and such was the swiftness and fury of her attack that her cutlass passed right into his side beneath his upraised arm before he had time to lower it. With a stupid look of surprise on his face he fell forward, and the thrust of his heavy body was too much for her to be able to withdraw her blade.

The other mutineers, who had fallen back a moment in amazement, sprang forward as she went down beneath the dead man, but Raoul and Red Lear were alongside and fired into the advancing wave that broke, and stayed again. She was on her feet in a moment, drawing and cocking her pistol. As she fired it an answering shot came, but went wide, and Jacky heard again what he knew so well by now, the strange soft sighing of a bullet past his ear. For a few minutes the fight became a hand-to-hand struggle ; Red Lear's knife rose and fell, and Raoul, with a strength no one would have guessed lay hid in his slim body, bore a man down to the deck, and kneeling on his chest, shot him at close range. Sophy had shot the man who had hurled himself at her, and was stooping down to pick up a cutlass from the deck, when the second mate, a thin, villainous-looking Brazilian, rushed to attack her. Jacky hurled himself at him, and laid hold of him after the manner of the Cornish wrestlers, holding fast to his shirt as a wrestler to his opponent's linen jacket. They swayed back and forth on the slippery deck, the Brazilian writhing like a wild cat, but Jacky got a good grip, and exerting all his skill, flung him clear over his shoulder in the fall known as the " Flying Mare." The man hit the deck with the back of his head and lay still.

" Well done for a proper Cornishman ! " yelled Red Lear, and himself discharged his pistol into the men, who broke and fell back to the ladders. Sophy, tall and terrifying, her breast covered with blood from the dead carpenter, came at them again, and they scrambled for the ladders and hung there like clustered flies. There was a breathing space then, for both sides were past the first frenzy, and suddenly one of the men began to howl and point.

" A bitch ! A bitch ! God !—look at her ! "

Sophy, cutlass in hand, came jeering at them, her harsh laughter killing theirs. She hung over the break of the poop and mocked at them.

" Yes ; that 's what you 've been afraid of all these years ! A woman ! A woman ! Brave fellows ! God damn you all for lousy sogers, you 've been afraid of a woman, and, by God, you will be again ! "

Jacky, his heart in his mouth, watched her, dishevelled, jeering, blowsy, all the authority that these cut-throats had bowed to and trembled at, gone with her man's gear, but her eyes flaming

and her wild head out-thrust, laughing at them.
And slowly they fell back from her jeers as they
had from her onslaught. She looked like one
armed with some stranger power than the ordinary
weapons of mankind ; fire seemed to spring from
her urgent body. A mutineer gave a sheepish
laugh, and then all the men gathered together in
the waist and began to talk and argue among themselves. They were still greatly in excess as far as
numbers went, but they were no longer as certain
of victory as they had been when the fumes of rum
mounted in their heads. The few on the poop had
the advantage of position, and the ringleaders—the
second mate and the carpenter—were dead.

A fragile peace, thin and brittle as glass, came to
the bloodstained quarter-deck for a few minutes.
They reloaded their pistols and consulted together.
It was a calm night, with only a light breeze from
the south—one of the fugitive airs that blow from
all points of the compass in those waters in the
summer months—and the *Moonraker* was gliding
along before it. Jacky had been dimly aware that
throughout the fighting there had been a man at
the wheel, and took it for granted that it could not
be a mutineer. Now the man spoke, and he
realised that it was Bristol Joe, a quiet fellow, whom
he had always been amazed at for a pleasant and
amiable pirate. Bristol Joe gave the wheel a little
spin, for the vessel had fallen off a few points
while he watched the struggle, and observed in a

mild voice : " That 's the worst of the trouble over, Captain, I du think." He rolled his quid in his cheek and fell to chewing.

But Bristol Joe spoke too soon. There came a crash from the hatch of the companion, and it was slammed to by a man from below, and though Raoul sprang to it and tried to wrench it open, it was too well secured. " The women ! " cried Raoul, " the women ! " And he made for the break of the poop. Red Lear flung himself in the way and held him back. " You 'll get your throat slit if you go down there, you young fool, and then what good 'll you be to them ? " Raoul struggled with him, but suddenly slipped to the deck, and it was seen that blood was pouring from an injury to his shoulder.

Sophy took a knife and cut the hem off her silken skirts, and bound up the wound with quick skilful fingers, and Raoul began to try and get to his feet again. Suddenly Jacky caught a soft whisper of " Massa ! Massa ! " He turned, to see the black face of Pete, the Jamaican cook, peering over the rail. He must have gone overboard and floated aft, and then hauled himself up by a rope hanging over the side. He saw Jacky looking at him and called out softly : " Jacky, Jacky, I beg you tell the Captain me one berry good nigger. Dem done shut me into de galley, but me bruk out wid de axe. Doa'n shoot if dis nigger come aboard." He splayed out his great fingers over the rail, and vaulting over, landed on the deck as softly as a cat ; the sea water ran off him and formed a pool. He saluted the Captain without a tremor of surprise visible in his dusky countenance, and said urgently : " De men, dem puttin' a bar'l gunpowder into de cabin below, sah. Dem is fixin' one long fuse."

CHAPTER XXV

IN WHICH JACKY LOOKS HIS LAST AT THE "MOONRAKER"

CAPTAIN SOPHY took a lantern and walked over to the break of the poop and stood holding the light so that it shone full upon her, a target indeed had not the very boldness of the action protected her. The men crowded in the waist stared at her, but not one raised a weapon, though an uneasy murmur ran through them.

"You lousy swine," said Sophy, "so you think you can blow me up, do you? If you blew yourselves up you 'd get nearer heaven than you ever will otherwise. Isn't there one of you with the sense of a weevil, that can step out like a man and speak up?"

The men muttered together, and then called to some one down the alleyway. He came out, a thin rat-faced fellow, with one eye and a scar right across his cheek. Jacky saw that he was one George, that the Captain had often cursed for a damned sea-lawyer.

"We 've had enough of you and your soft ways," he called up insolently, "and enough of your fancy lads and wenches. You can all go to hell together out of this."

"My soft ways may send you to hell first," said Sophy, in a sort of deadly pleasant voice, very quiet.

" You 've always been a fool, and you 've turned the other men into fools to match you. Without me you 'll be no better than a parcel of sogers. The first merchantman you meet 'll make one mouthful of you, and then it 'll be the yardarm for every son of a gun left alive. Not a man amongst you can navigate, and not one can keep off the rum unless he 's forced to. Set a light to the fuse and be damned to you. I shan't have to wait long till you all follow. What are you waiting for, my beauties ? "

There came snatches of sentences from the men, they talked together uneasily. One called out : " Us don't want to get rid of 'ee, Cap'n, if you 'd be as you used, and bring us to good loot. It 's your packet o' sissies us can't abide. Get rid of them and we 'll turn to again." Then Sophy began to swear very horribly and softly, worse than Jacky had ever heard her. She told them that it was not for them to make terms, and she drew a picture of their fate enough to curdle the blood. It was plain that the men, now the fire of the rum was out of them, began to feel they had been over hasty. George still was sullen, and again demanded that the passengers should be got rid of, and this the men all seconded. Sophy replied that as long as the ladies were still shut in below, in the next cabin to a barrel of gunpowder, she would not even talk about it. Bring them up to the poop and she might listen. Again the

men consulted, and then one disappeared down
the alleyway. Jacky could see Raoul forcing
himself to keep quiet, but with his hands clenched
so that the knuckles shone leper-white in the light
of the lantern. Then the two women appeared
below, both very composed though pale. The man
drew back sullenly to allow them to mount the
ladder. Raoul kept back in obedience to the
Captain's gesture, but Laura came to him and fell
into his arms with a little sob.

"You are alive! You are alive! Oh, it was
awful knowing nothing! Are they going to kill
us ?"

"I don't know." Raoul put his arm round
her and held her, and Mrs. Pounsell took
her other hand. They all stood quietly waiting.
Jacky drew closer to the break of the poop; he
wanted to miss nothing of the argufying. Red
Lear whispered urgently to the Captain : "You
must do what they say. Turn 'em off in a boat
with plenty of grub, they'll come to no harm."
Sophy slightly turned her head and looked at Red
Lear, who fell silent.

"Now that barrel of gunpowder," ordered the
Captain. "Up here on the poop. Lay aft and
fetch that barrel." The barrel, too, was brought
and stood on the poop. Laura stared at the dark
powder it contained in horrified fascination.

"Get out the longboat," ordered Sophy. Now
the men worked with a will, placing in the boat

all Sophy ordered—a compass, two breakers of
water and one of wine, a bunch of bananas, a bag
of biscuits, and some dried meats. Then the
boat was lowered, and towed gently alongside,
for the *Moonraker* was hardly moving in the
light air. Sophy ordered a man to get in and
step the mast and set the lugsail.

"Now," said the Captain, "over you get, Pete.
You go with them."

Pete, with a comic look of surprise on his black
face, clambered over, willing enough. The Captain
turned to Red Lear. "Now you," she said. Red
Lear started violently, and stood gazing, mouth
open. "You too," repeated the Captain. Red
Lear said in a low voice, "No, Sophy, no." The
Captain's face changed horribly in the light of the
lantern, became crimsoned with some strange
violence. "Would you set an example of dis-
obedience before these bloody mutineers? By
Christ, Red Lear, if you do that I will shoot you
like a dog." And Sophy levelled her pistol at
Red Lear's breast. Red Lear looked suddenly
an old man. His face seemed to go all soft and
broken, as though it were crumbling like the face
of an ancient corpse exposed to the air. He
shambled blindly down the ladder into the waist
and climbed over the ship's side.

Sophy turned to the women. "Now you."
Laura hesitated, looking very straightly at Sophy.
"He is coming too, I promise you," said Sophy,

with a dry smile. Then both ladies went, very
quietly. Sophy nodded at Jacky.

" Over you go, my lad. No desertion this time.
Stick to the sea, but don't take to piracy. You 're
too squeamish for that trade. But all the same,
you 'll be a man before I will ! "

Jacky said : " Let me stay." He knew that he
did not want to, that he was thankful to be leaving
the beautiful but wicked *Moonraker*, whose crimes
lay so thick upon her. Yet he hated going, he
knew not why. Sophy took his hand and looked
at him very kindly, but she shook her head. Then
she turned to Raoul, and Jacky drew back to the
break of the poop.

" My father, in the days when he was a preacher,
would have said : ' God go with you,' " she said.
" That 's not for the likes of me to say. Remember
me to your black General if you contrive to get to
him again. No one is stronger than Fate, Raoul.
Not your black Boney, or Boney himself. Not
even I."

Raoul said : " I shall not leave you on this
vessel." She looked at him sadly. " You must
go and quickly, while I can still hold them." This
time it was Raoul who shook his head. " You
can't stay here with these men." She broke into
a laugh.

" You fear for me now they know I am a woman ?
Believe me, there will be no danger from that. I
am not attractive as a woman ! No—not even to

such low fellows as these. It will make them hate and resent me, that is all."

" Then I shall not leave you to their anger," said Raoul obstinately. The men began to murmur at the delay, and Sophy turned and cursed at them, and they fell silent.

" They won't dare touch me ; they have no navigator since the second mate was killed. Besides, I have a method to master them that will not fail," she said, " have no fear. It is only by staying now that you are placing me in danger."

" Then you must come with us," said Raoul. She stared at him in amazement. " Come with you ? For what, pray ? That I may hang, and my body swing in chains, or if I escape that, to sit on shore and take to plain sewing ? No, I stand by my vessel."

" Then I stay," said Raoul. " They will doubtless kill me, but I cannot leave a woman, and one who has done so much for me, with these ruffians. Red Lear can lay a course and will protect those others till they are picked up."

There was a great softening of her look for the first time. " Listen, Raoul, I will tell you what you can do. Lay a mile off in the longboat for half an hour, and then you may put back for me and take me off if you still wish to. I swear to you I will not sail away, and I have never broken my word. See, the wind would not let me even if I would."

Raoul searched her eyes, but there was no trace

of falsehood in them. He kissed her hand on which the blood was hardly dry, and then he brushed past Jacky without heeding him, and went quickly down the ladder. Jacky followed, and they both got into the longboat.

Sophy called to them to use the oars, and Jacky, Raoul, and Pete began to row strongly away, Red Lear steering and holding the sheet of the sail. A current of air came over the surface of the water, and the sail filled and the longboat drew swiftly away. The moon had set, and it was by now very dark save for the brilliant and thickly-strewn stars. Those in the longboat saw Sophy come to the rail and stand holding up the lantern as if in farewell. They saw her open the door of the lantern, as though to reassure Raoul by the steadiness of the flame that she could not sail away. Then she faced the men, and her voice as she rapped out a command to them came clearly over the water. She ordered them upon the poop to pile their weapons there in token of submission. Red Lear gave a chuckle that seemed of pride, the first sign he had given of life, for he had taken the tiller like a man in a dream.

Suddenly Red Lear gave a high thin cry. It was all over so quickly that it seemed some sense other than sight must have warned him. One moment they saw Sophy standing, the open lantern held high, and the next she had dashed it into the barrel of gunpowder. There came a roar and a blinding light that flared to the heavens, and every soul gathered upon the poop of the *Moonraker* was blown into fiery fragments against the skies.

Then a thick darkness, lit only by showering sparks, like the dancing of fireflies, shut down over the sea.

CHAPTER XXVI

IN WHICH JACKY GROWS UP

THE darkness began to be broken by flickering lights, flames that swelled and ran together and presently leapt from the *Moonraker's* hull up her rigging, till she was a roaring furnace. All night long she burned, and those in the longboat sailed about and about lest they could pick up any living creature, all but impossible as they knew it to be. Had the men not swarmed upon the poop at Sophy's command, it might well have chanced that far too many of the mutineers, alive and uninjured, would have been rescued to have been safe for that small craft with her law-abiding intentions. But the only man picked up with the breath of common humanity in him—few signs of it were left in his distorted shape—was one they could not even recognise. He died, his last gasp sighing through a mouth that was nothing but a broken cavern, at the pale hour of dawn, lying across a thwart with his blind eyes turned towards the blind heavens. Captain Sophy had taken her mutineers with her, and she had done it even as she had lived, without scruple. Only those she wished to save had she sent away.

The longboat was picked up next day by a Yankee trader, the *Martha P. Harris*, bound for Charleston, and four days later she delivered her chance pas-

156

sengers safe and unharmed at the quays of that flourishing city, where a discreet reticence veiled their tale, for the sake of Red Lear and Pete.

But it would have mattered little to Red Lear what they had told of him or the *Moonraker*. He died, weeping bitterly into a softer pillow than he had ever known, in a kindly house in Charleston, a day later. His wandering talk was all of God and the devil, and of how hard it was to know what the Lord meant a man to do for the best.

Indeed, as Raoul pointed out to Jacky, that was a hard question, almost as hard as deciding with what nation the Lord sided. All invoked Him, to Him were the victorious indebted ; with Him did the vanquished condole, while realising it must be part of the Divine scheme that His own nation should thus be tried by a temporary set-back. It might even be that He was on all sides and yet on none ; and all that a man could be sure of was that he had to fight for whatever was best worth it. It was only if he began to wonder if anything were worth fighting for that he was damned indeed.

The light-hearted and untroubled Pete attached himself to Raoul as servant, and went to France with him. Jacky got a ship for Liverpool, and from there a coasting schooner to Plymouth, and so he saw again the green slopes of the bay, so gentle and smooth after the heights of San Domingo, and, some ten months after leaving it, came back

to the house in Saltash.   He found his father well,
but old Tamsin True had died after a blow from
a stone thrown at her from behind a hedge.   Jacky
thought it was better to be a witch in San Domingo
than in Saltash.

Jacky and Raoul wrote to each other during the
years that followed, but what with England and
France being at war again, and England and
America going to war, they did not meet for twenty
years, not till the great Boney had died on rock-
bound St. Helena.   Jacky had sailed the seven
seas of the world by then, and one of his voyages
had taken him again to the towering green mountains of that island which had been new-christened
Haiti.

Then came the day when Jacky sailed into Massa-
chusetts Bay, commander and part-owner of a
lovely vessel, the *Balkis* : and, stuns'ls and skys'ls
set, foamed up to the river on the top of the tide.
Raoul, top-hatted, even as Jacky was himself, met
him at the quay.   That was a queer meeting.
They were two prosperous middle-aged men,
but as hands and eyes met, the years fell away,
and it was as though they were back again in the
fantastic days of San Domingo.   But Jacky was
never quite sure after that first evening in the
stately Boston house, shaded by elm-trees, that
Miss Laura was really glad to see him again.   Could
it be that she would not be glad of anything that
recalled Captain Sophy ?   They did not talk of the

Moonraker, however, until they were alone. They talked of Toussaint, the most unhappy of men.

Raoul told of the lonely fortress near Besançon, and of the unanswered letters to the First Consul ; he told of him that last winter morning when, dead from starvation, the black General had been found lying with his grey head leaning forward on a cold and empty stove, his teeth all fallen out, and his limbs distorted with rheumatism.

Toussaint's predictions had come true, and frightful massacres of the whites had followed Leclerc's breach of faith to him ; and equally fearful massacres of the blacks, who were penned in arenas and torn to pieces by specially imported bloodhounds.

Leclerc brought back slavery and the slave-trade, but he was fighting a losing battle, rebellion and disease both grew throughout the Island. Leclerc died of fever, and the beautiful Pauline sailed away, and the English blockaded the island and prevented supplies getting to the French troops. When the French finally were forced to surrender, they had lost over forty thousand of the finest and most gallant troops in the world, and ten thousand of skilled seamen, a loss felt bitterly by France two years later at Trafalgar. The last whites left in the island were most frightfully massacred by Dessalines, who for two years knew no limit to his lusts and cruelties. The man who had been born a savage, who had been forced to be a slave, became a general and ended an emperor. The only thing that he most ardently wished to attain and could not, in spite of taking everywhere with him a skilled dancing-master, was proficiency in the art of dancing. His atrocities brought him a tyrant's death from the knife of an assassin.

Christophe, the cold and resolute, came to power after him, and his rich imagination caused a great palace to be reared above the fateful Cape Francois. Like the Pyramids, it was built with blood and tears. Christophe grew in tyranny, and men hardly dared to breathe in the shadow that he cast. Jacky told Raoul of how Christophe, unusually gracious to him for old times' sake, took him over the splendid palace, and caused one of his young black soldiers to walk off the battlements into space, so as to show the white man the extent of his power. Christophe, fierce and proud to the last, did not await assassination, and when the end was in sight he bathed, dressed in fair linen, and killed himself, like the king that he was.

Men still shuddered at his name, said Jacky, but Toussaint, the pure and honest, was unsung, unvenerated ; everywhere through the Island it was the memory of the dancing butcher Dessalines that the blacks revered, because it was he who had turned out the whites. Jacky, looking at Raoul, thought of that high and fruitless adventure of his youth, when time and money had meant nothing, and he gave a sigh that was half for Raoul and half for himself.

Of the *Moonraker* the friends spoke little, but Jacky could see that, even at this lapse of time, Raoul was moved by the memory. Toussaint's fame would spread again amongst men, but all memory of Sophy, save in the hearts of Jacky and Raoul, was lost in the Atlantic waves. She had come and gone, leaving no visible trace behind her.

Jacky married a Salem girl and took her home to Saltash, where she made him a good wife. She bore him a son and daughter, whom he christened Toussaint and Sophia. But no one could pronounce the boy's rightful name, so he was always called John.

Jacky was a prosperous man, and as men go, happy; but often at night, when the wind was howling up the Tamar, and his wife said comfortably: "How good to be at home, and not at sea to-night!" then he would think of the *Moonraker* and the lovely way she met the waves, and of the great mountains and green forests of San Domingo. And he would see again in the bowl of troubled water which was his memory, a black face and a white one that was sun-reddened; and they were the faces of the two most real people he had ever known. He wondered whether it was because, in spite of their difference each from each, they both had always known what they were

after, or whether it was simply that he himself had
been younger and more eager. He would look
across at the goodly pink and white Salem woman,
and think she was as a puff of smoke from a cannon's
mouth fading away over the sea. And when he
thought that, he would get up, filled with remorse,
and go over and kiss his wife, and she would smile
at him, not knowing why he had kissed her.